Ferry Tales
from Puget Sound

A Collection of Stories, Poems & Anecdotes

Editor: Joyce Delbridge
Poetry Editor: Nancy Rekow
Art Editor: Elizabeth Zwick

Elizabeth Zwick

Vashon Point Productions
Vashon Island, WA

Greg Onewein, Bainbridge Island, WA

Copyright © 1986 by Vashon Point Productions
All rights for individual writing and artwork revert to the writers and artists.

International Standard Book Number: 0-9616103-0-1
Library of Congress Catalog Card Number: 86-50007

Cover design by Elizabeth Zwick

Printed by Enterprise Graphics

For additional copies or information:

Vashon Point Productions
Joyce Delbridge, Editor
Rt. 1, Box 432
Vashon Island, WA 98070

(206) 567-4829

Dedicated to my grandchildren
who become ferry watchers when they visit my island

Michael Delbridge
Brandy Elliott
Joshua Delbridge
Alexis Delbridge

Greg Onewein, Bainbridge Island, WA

Acknowledgments

Without the help of many people, my dream of producing an entertaining book about ferry experiences could never have happened.

My husband, Bill, has backed me every step of the way throughout my writing career and the long creation of *Ferry Tales*. His advice has been invaluable.

So many writers and artists submitted material for *Ferry Tales* that there wasn't room in this first book to use it all. For future publications, we ask writers to continue sending us stories through **Vashon Point Productions**. We prefer short pieces, 1,000 words or less, about happenings on the ferries. We also would like to hear from interested artists.

As *Ferry Tales* goes to press, I thank Zola Ross for her tutelage and encouragement when I ended my teaching career and started a writing career in 1979.

Nightwriters of Vashon, a professional writing group, initiated the writing contest that brought in the first stories. Members were Hunter Davis, Gaylen Gregory, Reva Sparkes, Neil Fridley, Kathryn Park Brown, Erica Mead, Mary Young Bizzell, and Josh Webster.

Pacific Northwest Writers Conference sponsored our contest in Spring, 1985, and placed our quest for material before their members. Evelyn McKay of Vashon guided our steps, Amos Wood of Mercer Island opened doors, and Gladys Nelson of Seattle helped in many ways.

After I decided to carry out the publication of *Ferry Tales*, I received wise, caring, essential help from Nancy Rekow, book consultant, and Elizabeth Zwick, Art Editor. They have guided the project to fruition.

Pat Patterson, Public Relations Director of Washington State Ferries, circulated our flyers for material and kept ferry workers informed about the publication. Kay Walsh, Editor of the magazine *Waterlines*, published the winning pieces from our PNWC contest.

Ferry workers, current and retired, gave me interviews, providing background information and stories. Many friends gave me their anecdotes to write.

Ruth Eggleston, Carol and John Pearson, and Barbara Robbins helped with proofreading. Mary Brown and Margi Berger helped with typing.

I thank them all. And last, I thank my mother, Ruby Watford, who through her diaries and newspaper articles introduced me to writing as a way of expressing feelings.

Joyce Delbridge, Vashon Island, WA

Table of Contents

9	Foreword	Joyce Delbridge
11	From Alex's Philippine Cafe	Jerry-Mac Johnston
11	Early Monday Morning	as told by Margaret Philbrick
12	As the Ferry Churns	Lauran Cole
14	Ferry to Cattle Point	Linda Andrews
14	What's the Hurry?	Robert D. Johnson
15	Hot Mop	Steve Saul
15	The Riot Act	Robert D. Johnson
16	Professional Ferry Patron	Bill Speidel
17	How can such hulks of iron and steel	Winifred Jaeger
18	Coal Oil Cuge	Jacqueline Flothe Hillstrom
20	The 2:10 Ferry	Harriet O. Davis
21	Echo Navigation	Morris H. Pixley
22	A Perfect Day for Sailing	Harry Proctor
24	After the Ferry Ride	Catharine Hoffman Beyer
25	First Ferry	Peter L. Smith
26	Ferry Names on Puget Sound	Margaret D. McGee
28	The Rambling Pram	Reva Sparkes
29	Oh, Captain	Peggy Julian
29	Overslept	as told by Betty Gleason
30	9 to 5	Paul Halvorson
30	November from the Ferryboat *Spokane*	Margi Berger
31	Muckelshoot Ferry	Fredrick Zydek
32	Night Ride to Orcas	Eric Perret
36	Slithering Silvers!	Mike Skalley
36	Line-up	Richard B. Braden
37	Speedy	as told by Captain Zak Farid
38	A Ferry Affair	Janet Lonergan
39	Issy	as told by Asta Schade
40	You're the One Who's Worried	Joyce Delbridge
41	A Very Special Problem	Robert D. Johnson
42	Shiners	Robert H. Redding
44	The Mating of the *Hyak*	Hal B. Fernandez
45	Cartwheeling	Kris Hutchison
45	*Walla Walla* at Night	Sara Rekow
46	The Ferry That Will Live Forever	Kathryn E. White
49	Elegy for the *Vashon*	Tom Snyder
50	Crossing Water	David B. McCreary
51	The Boy Who Wandered Around	Kerry Godes
52	The Storm	Jean Isabelle Iverson
53	Toot, Toot, Toot, Toot, Toot	Captain Glen Willers
54	Stress! Does It Ride With You?	Steele Coddington

55	A Proper Banker	*as told by Bill Mish*
57	Quinault George	*as told by Captain Ted Olson*
58	A Merry Ride to the Ferry	*Richard M. West*
60	Commuting	*C. Hunter Davis*
60	Twenty Cars Too Late	*Richard B. Braden*
61	High School Commuting on the *Crosline*	*Howard White*
62	Quiet! Please	*Robert Mize*
62	Wanna Bet?	*as told by Jack Pennington*
63	Quarters	*as told by Dorothy Jones*
64	Never Underestimate the Ladies' Room	*Blanche Caffiere*
66	A Dollar a Hog, 50 Cents More for a Man	*R. Wayne Strack*
67	A Good Boat	*Robert D. Johnson*
68	Dismissal on the Seattle to Winslow Ferry Run	*Susan Landgraf*
69	Plans	*Linda A. Vandlac*
70	Last Ferry	*John Damon*
73	Departure	*Lonny Kaneko*
74	The Host	*Len Elliott*
74	Vashon Hot Heads	*Roland Carey*
75	The Popcorn Caper	*Garland Baker Norin*
75	Whistles	*Captain Glen Willers*
76	Tolkein Rides the Ferry	*Frank Jackson*
77	Landings	*Captain Glen Willers*
77	Shaw Island Landing	*Joan Bellinger*
78	The Honeymoon	*Kathryn Park Brown*
80	The Blink of an Eye	*Marybelle Craig*
81	Clyde	*Peter Fromm*
82	Night Ferry	*Wilkes 5th graders, Bainbridge Is.*
84	Jasmine	*Tressa AspiriHakala*
85	Ferry Unlikely	*Mary M. Webber*
85	On a Slow Ferry to Victoria	*Sharon Hashimoto*
86	Who Needs the Ferries	*Junius Rochester*
87	What the Captain Does	*Mike Skalley*
88	The Last Crossing	*Larry Johnson*
90	Keys!	*Martha M. Richards*
90	A Cluster of Grapes	*as told by Joan Wickham*
91	San Juan Tail	*Jessie Winn*
91	Babysitting on Puget Sound	*Mae Swofford*
92	Letting Go	*Janet Appleton*
94	Elegy Without Grief	*Judith Skillman*
95	Missing the Ferry	*Lee Dhyan Owens*
97	Journeys	*C. Hunter Davis*
98	Fitting	*Tom Erdmann, Jr.*
100	Contributors' Notes	

Table of Illustrations

Ann Alexander — page 85
Darsie Beck — page 47
Knute Berger — page 37
Michael DeVoe — page 56
Jacqueline Flothe Hillstrom — page 19
Jon Rader Jarvis — page 96
Hannah Jones — page 31
Judith Lawrence (J.L.) — pages 9, 11, 17, 39, 43, 61, 66, 69, 77, 78, 84, 91, 98
Mary Macapia — page 25
Sharon Munger — page 65
Greg Onewein — pages 2, 4, 21, 22, 53, 67, 72
Hita von Mende — pages 83, 88
Susan Wallace — pages 13, 15, 35, 41, 63, 99
George Wright — page 95
Elizabeth Zwick — pages 10, 32

Judith Lawrence, Vashon Island, WA

Foreword

I am a ferry watcher. Ferries pass my window, gliding back and forth between Vashon and Southworth, their white and green bulks stately, impassive. Not until I lift my binoculars do I see people.

People on the ferries. That's what this book is about. It trains the binoculars on commuters from Vashon, Bainbridge, Port Townsend, Seattle, the San Juans, and on the dry land tourists from everywhere.

Most of these stories are real life experiences, like the time Harry Proctor's boat lay swamped between the ferry and Southworth dock. Some, like Larry Johnson's story of the captain on his last day before retirement, are imaginative. Others, like Kathy White's rendezvous with the *Vashon*, are nostalgic. Poems brush word pictures of events or emotions behind relationships, as in Catharine Beyer's "After the Ferry Ride." Anecdotes focus on frequent or strange ferry incidents as in Richard Braden's account of the irate commuter who missed the ferry or Steve Saul's unusual yarn of a happening below decks. Artwork catches a scene, as in Jon Jarvis's picture of two young girls staring in awe when the noisy *Kalakala* passes them on an island beach.

Writers and artists throughout Puget Sound responded to our request for material about happenings on the ferries. Their response revealed a wealth of stories. We envision another collection, another publication. This, then, is our first book of *Ferry Tales* from the great inland sea of the West, Puget Sound.

Joyce Delbridge, Vashon Island, WA

Elizabeth Zwick, Bainbridge Island, WA

From Alex's Philippine Cafe

Everything is stillborn
   mornings on
     the waterfront

The mist mates with
  the bay
     giving slow birth
     to the first
     ferry from
     Bainbridge
And the day is alive

Jerry-Mac Johnston, Seattle, WA

Early Monday Morning

On the first morning of his new job in Seattle, Anthony drove bleary-eyed onto the ferry from Orcas Island. How would he ever manage to meet this crack-of-dawn schedule?

Parked next to him on the ferry was a Chrysler. Anthony watched the driver surreptitiously. First the man poured a cup of coffee from his thermos and placed it on the dash. Next he plugged his shaver into the cigarette lighter and shaved between gulps of coffee. Then he opened the glove compartment. Out came a covered plastic bowl of steaming hot cereal. Finally, cereal bowl empty, coffee drunk, and shaver stored away, he pulled out toothbrush and toothpaste and headed for the men's room.

Anthony stretched back in his seat with a grin of relief. He had his answer.

Told to the Editor by Margaret Philbrick, Orcas Island, WA

As the Ferry Churns

It used to be my playground; now I just watch the kids a lot. It's hard not to, in a contained space where noise carries and where rows and rows of back-to-back seats provide more gymnastic apparatus than a playground.

It took me a long time to get as brave as the kids I watch now. My first few ferry rides were spent as far away from the window as possible, gripping the edge of the seat so I wouldn't fall off and drown. I was somewhere around four years old, my little sister about two. She used to scare me to death when she not only jumped on the seats, jarring *my* perch, but ran up and down the aisles as if the floor would hold her up.

It didn't take long, of course, until that confidence infected me, until I darted around corners fast enough, more than once, to plunge straight into a newly-primped woman coming out of the Ladies' Room.

Late night trips were especially fun with fellow passengers few and far between. We could climb over the top of one seat, right onto the one facing the opposite direction in the next pair, jump over the gap between seats and repeat the process, for a long way down the boat. Inevitably, though, some workman with his lunch bucket tucked under his arm would be stretched out along the length of a padded seat, snoozing. We wouldn't see him until we landed on top of him.

They still do the same things I did. But now, they're usually pests. Once in a while a cute one will wander up to me, interrupting my reflections, with eyes wide enough, step uncertain enough, that I want to solve her mystery and show her big people don't always bite. And I'm still not too old to recall the wrath of an embarrassed parent. I make it a point to smile at the ones who come to fetch *their* kids off a sleepy me.

I watch the parents, too. Perhaps because it's closing in on me, the expectation that I'll soon have a brood of my own. But those worn-out ferry mothers do little to inspire maternity. Constant energy output, no time for reflection. So this is what the early years of adventure and exploration and education are all about, I think—to eventually have to quell any further personal reaching, to narrow the ambitions of a mind so carefully nurtured for width, in the interest of raising others to the same important end.

But last week was different. Another ferry ride home and, as they usually are now, it was for a special occasion. My sister was coming home after months in Alaska. With her new husband. Newly pregnant.

I couldn't help it. I was beaming. The anticipation of a new life, a person as precious to me as my sister, was an excitement reaching further than any I had ever experienced. Maybe those three little imps tagging after the bored-looking couple who walked past us were more than just a burden to their parents. Maybe. It's still hard to tell when they're just strangers on the Ferry.

But my niece or nephew—I'll race him or her over the seats!

Lauran Cole, Bainbridge Island, WA

Susan Wallace, Bainbridge Island, WA

Ferry to Cattle Point

Without welcome
the ferryman waves us
onto the iron deck.
He signs his own dialect,
linking stranger to stranger
with a chain of suggestions.

His palms meet
as if in prayer
to show us how close
and because we're floating
we mind him like children,
and pretend there's efficiency
in being close.

We keep trying
till he signals approval
and blocks the tires
for no turning back,
our security vested
in a piece of wood.

Each hand controls
a line of machines
he knows will obey
as he charts our passage
from concrete to concrete
through a slippery
interlude of trust.

Linda Andrews, Kirkland, WA

What's the Hurry?

It happened at Orcas on the ferry *Klickitat* one day after sunset. We saw headlights approaching from up the road. A passenger erupted from the car, ran the full length of the dock, and in spite of our yells jumped onto the deck of the ferry.

As the deckhand picked the ferry patron up, he said, "What's your hurry, son? The boat's just comin' in."

Robert D. Johnson, Clallam Bay, WA

Hot Mop

The only fire I've seen on the ferries happened to yours truly.

We use hydrogen peroxide to treat the sewage tanks. But industrial strength, the kind we use, is dangerous. With enough air, it can ignite spontaneously.

One day a drum of the stuff sprang a leak, so the crew had all this hydrogen peroxide spilled below the car deck. They took a mop, several mops in fact, to clean it up. When they finished their watch they thought they had taken care of it all.

First thing I noticed when I came on watch was that the entire Number Two engine room was filled with smoke. It didn't smell like anything I'd ever smelled before—not electrical, not machinery—I couldn't tell what. It just smelled like rags burning. Sure enough, one of the mops was blazing away.

I don't know why the automatic CO^2 system didn't go off. It should have. Anyway, I stuck the mop in a garbage can to smother the fire, and went to the other engine room to tell the chief. By the time I came back, the mop had re-ignited. So I took the thing and put it in a bucket of water.

But, like the trick birthday candle you blow on and it won't go out, the mop wouldn't go out. There was just enough of the mop sticking out above the water to re-ignite.

That did it. I yanked the mop out of the bucket and heaved it overboard. There was enough water in Puget Sound to put out the fire.

Steve Saul, Vashon Island, WA

The Riot Act

One day Denny was sitting in his usual spot in the galley on the *Nisqually*. He wore his regular uniform—black pants, white shirt and a black tie.

A woman passenger came up and began to read him the riot act, complaining about the poor ferry service, the late sailing, and on and on. Denny tried to interrupt several times, but the woman would not listen. Finally, she ran out of things to say.

Denny responded, "Ma'am, I agree. I wish there was something I could do, but I'm just the bread truck driver."

Robert D. Johnson, Clallam Bay, WA

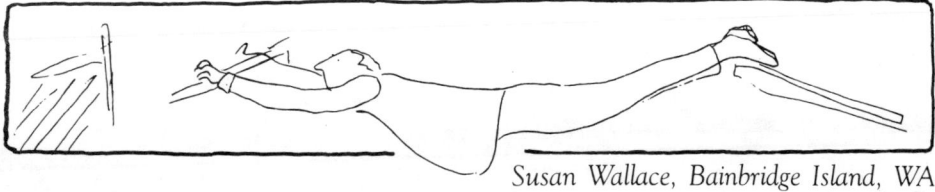

Susan Wallace, Bainbridge Island, WA

Professional Ferry Patron

The human relationship between the operators of the Washington State Ferry System and its regular patrons is unlike any other on the face of the globe . . . and reminds us more than anything else of the old woman who lived in a shoe taking care of all those obnoxious kids, or perhaps a mother hen with a bunch of chicks: She doesn't want anything harmful to occur, but sometimes they drive her right out of her mind . . . .

The entire operation is geared to the poorest-paying customer of the bunch—the guy we call the Professional Ferry Patron. He's the one who rides on the commuter ticket. You may not realize this, but he "owns" the ferry that he rides on. And while the State may run it for him and pay all the bills, it's his private yacht. And periodically, the State must be jacked up and "put down," a feat that requires unending dexterity on the part of the Professional Ferry Patron. However, he has plenty of time, energy and enthusiasm for this pursuit . . . which allows him to vent his spleen without getting fired from his regular job.

Professional Ferry Patrons have one common denominator: an abiding conviction that the Washington State Ferry System always is wrong . . . .

The PFP has no admiration for the Amateur Ferry Rider like you. You don't have the right change. You don't know which is the right lane. You don't know where you're going when you get off the ferry. And you don't know how to drive aggressively when you're on it. You are the reason why the speed limit on board a Washington State Ferry is only 5 miles an hour . . . .

The PFPs established control of the situation immediately after the State took over the privately-owned system in 1951. Historically, the Black Ball people had given one long and two short toots when their ferries approached a landing, and the State had the temerity to change it to two even toots.

The howl that went up was heard around the world . . . .

Well, at least around the Sound.

Want to know how that one came out? Listen for the "tooot toot-toot" of the tooter when your ferry toots for her landing at Winslow.

Excerpt from Wet Side of the Mountain
by Bill Speidel, Vashon Island, WA

Judith Lawrence, Vashon Island, WA

How can such hulks of iron and steel

with endless array of engines and gear
clanking, thumping, banging,
ramming the pilings till they squirm and squeak,
churning the water into salty spray,
alarming the fishes (but never the gulls),
shuddering until the brains of passengers jiggle,
bumping the tires of trucks and trailers, buses and bicycles,
all swallowed up into the cavernous holds;

how can these bulky creatures
seem to glide in the distance
stately in their white elegance,
patiently weaving and reweaving
paths across the Sound,
making even more perfect
the mountains, islands and skylines
until, at the end of day,
they silently tread the dark surface
on a thousand feet of light.

Winifred Jaeger, Kirkland, WA

Coal Oil Cuge

My grandfather's brother John Rauen, a long time Vashon Island resident, was a daily customer on the Tacoma-Tahlequah ferry run. Uncle John, probably South Vashon's uncontested local character, was better known to my family as Coal Oil Cuge. The coal oil part of his name came from Uncle Cuge's habit of dousing his kitchen wood stove, hot or cold, with kerosene for a lively start. The stove lids and big tea kettle always rose to the occasion.

Back then, in the 30's and 40's, the ferries were small, simple vessels with their usual ferry problems, but somehow I feel certain that Uncle Cuge added to their daily concerns. He drove a Model A Ford and would always lead the pack of cars on and off the deck. This feat he accomplished by leaving home or work early and driving in second gear.

Cuge was never a man of great ambitions or ever wasted motion on the non-essentials of life. He did not like to shift gears so he always kept to a steady second gear pace, come stop signs, red lights or high water. Invariably he collected a mile-long line of cars behind him on the way to the ferry. Fortunately, in those days the island folks were a patient and long suffering lot. But even at the tender age of five, my older brother and I sat in Uncle Cuge's car feeling awkward with the horns honking and the curious stares we always received.

Our most exciting trips were of course in the rough weather. Cuge would get his four hand-rolled Bull Durham cigarettes stacked up on his ears (two on each side), pull his old gray tweed flat topcap down to keep everything in place, give the Ford a crank, check his pocket watch, and away we would go, off to the ferry in second gear.

Mother and Dad and our beloved dog Whimpy came behind in the family car. Whenever I looked, Dad always seemed to be holding back a laugh as the parade of cars began to collect behind us. Even Whimpy would poke his head out the window with a wide grin on his face.

Upon boarding the ferry I'd know we were in for a rough trip when not only were the chocks thrown carefully under the car but the cars were also tied down and everyone was ordered above the car deck.

Calmer times, my brother and I got to ride in the pilot's house and steer our great vessel. My brother steered with a glare in his eyes that would have made Captain Bly grow pale.

Landing the little ferries was always a difficult task at best as they were single screw, and with the tides and wind we would bang and crash our way into the slip, often backing off two or three times before finally landing. The pilings would rock and pitch crazily when suffering a direct hit. I'm sure the pilebucks who constantly replaced those pilings had the most secure jobs on Puget Sound. Dad suspected maybe the pilebucks also ran the ferries, but it was never confirmed.

We always watched excitedly for the pods of killer whales that were present in those days. It was "common knowledge" that these packs of sea monsters would immediately devour everyone on the ferry at first opportunity, and most likely the ferry itself. But upon my own investigation and much to my disappointment, I never could find anyone with a friend or relative who had succumbed to the dreaded whale.

Uncle Cuge's old place near Reddings Beach had a character all its own. A very old house when purchased, it never was brought up to any kind of modern standard except for the valiant attempts my father made on it. For my brother, me, and Whimpy, Uncle Cuge always welcomed our presence with an opened bag of donuts and boiled coffee.

My brother and I found the time to dig gunnysacks of clams, take the boat out for a row, and go swimming at Reddings Beach. Uncle Cuge generally supervised these activities from his old leather easy chair next to the kitchen stove, while he rested his laurels and rolled a supply of cigarettes. That chair contained a twenty-year supply of tobacco droppings and wheat papers, but then it kept everyone else from wanting to sit in his chair.

For Cuge, the crowning expectation of our visit was to finish the weekend off with my mother's clam chowder, along with her coveted chicken and dumplings. It was always a store-bought chicken as all of Uncle's chickens were his pets. Of course, as soon as any chicken's name was mentioned, that settled any further inquiries on my family's part. Thank heaven for my family that store-bought chickens were anonymous.

Uncle would be first to the table, carefully setting his false teeth next to his plate. This procedure was a never ending annoyance to all the relatives but apparently a great comfort to Cuge. Why anyone needed to remove his teeth to eat Mother's dumplings I'll never know.

These sumptuous Sunday dinners always ended with the announcement that we must make the last ferry. Even in those slower, simpler times, island living still ran according to the ferry schedule.

Jacqueline Flothe Hillstrom, Sequim, WA

Jacqueline Flothe Hillstrom, Sequim, WA

The 2:10 Ferry

On the Winslow run, the *Walla Walla*
with a light load
glides across the cavity of the afternoon.

Two women, too free to fret about their hair,
gray ruffs in the north wind,
trade the camera for a shot of each
against the retreating town.

A single sailboat up the Sound
tacks across to Shilshole.
A tug with a tow of sand
waits out the ebb.

On the upper deck inside, the retired couple
in ski coats that have never seen the slopes
read their paper, one half each.

Five workers from the Trident Base
move pegs along a cribbage board,
smoke and boast and chide.

Solitaries on the naugahyde seats inhabit islands
until the man coughing phlegm
leans across to the bench behind him
to say he's going to Veterans' next week
for surgery.

The ship shudders
around the buoy off Wing Point
and cuts power in Eagle Harbor
to run to Winslow dock.

Its deck crew move in boredom
throwing lines, squinting into the sun.
The passengers carry
inevitabilities ashore.

Harriet O. Davis, Seattle, WA

Greg Onewein, Bainbridge Island, WA

Echo Navigation

Before the days of radar, ferry captains trained themselves to reckon where their boats were in a fog by tooting the whistle and counting the seconds before they heard the echo. Echoes told them how close the dolphins were on each side so that the captain could bring the boat into port by steering between them.

Other information was important. For instance, if a whistle sound hit a solid wall, the echo would bounce back sharply. If it hit a ragged hillside, the echo was apt to sound just as ragged.

Even though captains revere the old steam whistle, they admit that a well designed airhorn gives a sharper echo. Now, with the use of radar, there is less need for echo navigation, but many captains still use echoes from their whistles (airhorn or steam) for dead reckoning.

Morris H. Pixley, Seattle, WA

Greg Onewein, Bainbridge Island, WA

A Perfect Day for Sailing

It was a perfect July day—gentle southerly breeze, sun warm on my back, sky so clear I could see the whole range of Olympic Mountains. We were anchored on the west side of Blake Island at the end of our annual single-handed overnighter. I had just cast off Captain Nemo and John Boy. They sailed lazily away around the south end of the island.

I hoisted Harlequin's anchor and drifted while raising the sails, then off to a quiet beat. The wind was steady. I trimmed the sails and braked down the helm, allowing my Ranger 33 to sail itself. Then I brought out a camera to capture the romance of the moment.

In a passing fancy, I thought it would be fun to have a picture of my sailboat from the dinghy—a picture of the sailboat sailing itself with nobody on board. Grabbing the camera, I stepped gingerly into Toad, my 9-foot Ranger Minto. With a gentle but firm tug we were in tow.

Chuckling with delight at such an innovative idea, I focused the camera, snapped the picture, and then stretched out on Toad to relax in the sun. We were sailing in the direction of the Southworth ferry landing.

Some time had passed when I heard a ferry rumbling in the distance. But that wasn't what caught my attention, even though we would eventually have crossed paths. I also heard gurgling water and a tugging at the bow line.

Sitting up, I realized the wind had shifted so that I was now on a collision course with the ferry. The wind speed had increased and so had my boat speed.

Moving to the bow of Toad, I grabbed the towline. I was surprised at how unstable the dinghy became with a 220-pound man in the bow being towed at almost five knots. Immediately the bow plunged underwater.

My body reacted without thought. I found myself in the back seat of the dinghy. A moment later 50 gallons of water flooded into the boat like a tidal wave, slamming the transom, knocking me off my feet and onto my shins and forearms. I moved to the center of Toad, balanced myself, and reached for the camera. The only thing I could do was stuff it into my mouth.

Just then I heard the ferry slow down. I had sailed in between the ferry and the Southworth landing. Now a unique problem faced me. The ferry passengers realized it too. They lined the deck, pointing in my direction.

My mouth ached and my teeth hurt from gripping the camera. I was trying to formulate a plan when the ferry insisted I hurry by letting out a blast that told everyone on the boat where this trip's entertainment was.

With a maniacal leap to the bow, I grabbed again for the tow line. It jerked from my grasp again and again. When I finally succeeded in holding it, I moved swiftly back to the center aft portion of Toad. The water in the boat hardly moved. Success! I pulled hand over hand. The bow of the dinghy raised, forcing me to stand up. I maneuvered in water-ski fashion, guiding Toad's bow toward the transom of the sailboat. The problem now increased in complexity. My body was nine feet away from Harlequin's stern pulpit. My muscles ached; my grip was slipping; a spasm hit my jaws clamped over the camera; the cold from the water was draining my strength. If I didn't move soon there wouldn't be a second chance.

Tenderly balanced, I jerked on the tow line, propelling myself forward to the stern pulpit. Toad slipped away, and my fingertip grip on the sailboat's pulpit lasted only a second before the icy water of Puget Sound closed over my legs.

For some reason unknown to me, my left hand found the backstay. Then I felt a pain down my chest and between my legs and realized I was saddle-style over the towing line. The water-filled dinghy whose towing weight must have been 500 pounds was pulling me up, urging me to get into the sailboat.

Somehow, I did.

I collapsed on my back in the cockpit and watched the ferry steer around me. People in the crowd at the railing cheered and applauded as they glided by. The camera dropped to the deck. There were teeth marks in the plastic.

The July sun warmed my body, the Olympics stood like sentinels on the horizon, and the southerly breeze rocked the boat gently. It was still a perfect day for sailing.

I have since mounted the photograph, and it hangs over the desk in my study to remind me of that faceless cheering section on the Fauntleroy Ferry.

Harry Proctor, Seattle, WA

After the Ferry Ride

The woman at the other table
is gray, wrinkled, and dressed
neatly in lemon linen. She sips Chablis
from a thin glass. As we are leaving
she leans forward, stops me
with a vein-mapped hand, and says, "Reminds me
of my misspent youth." I think
she means our children. Jessica and Emily
have been flapping like flags over the chairs
and the patio boards of the Kingston Inn
while Dick and I drink beer. They have borne our threats
with the gravity of seals playing in the bay.
I smile at the woman, but I do not ask.

The *Chelan* ferry sounds its old fart
horn, and we board for the return.
When the dock lifts its tongue, we float away.
Around us, the sails of smaller boats
fly colors at the sky. The sun
hangs like a grapefruit overhead, and my daughters shriek
and thump the deck as two killer whales
shine black and white arcs over water,
then dig deep shadows going down.

When we get back to Edmonds,
the sand is winking. Jessica and Emily
race for a pile of rocks good for climbing.
Agile and bright as kites, they curl toes
around wet gray stones. Dick and I toss
warnings and a yellow frisbee. The disc
hangs between us and cloud-lined sky
before I catch it. When I snap it back,
the question I forgot to ask is sour
on my tongue: Which of us were the shadows
of the woman's misspent youth?

Catharine Hoffman Beyer, Seattle, WA

Mary Macapia, Vashon Island, WA

First Ferry

In distant sunlight, white boat on black water
    wears a halo of mist.

Like the tines of a thousand combs,
    fir trees bristle on rakish headlands.

Heaving pilings, cormorant perch,
    open tarred arms to welcome our boat.

Peter L. Smith, Bellevue, WA

Yours, Margaret McBee

Ferry Names on Puget Sound

What's the best name for a new ferry?
The *Vacation State*, or the *Klahowya*?
The *Washington State*, or the *Tillikum*?
How about the *Sales-Tax State*, or the *Duckabush*?

If it weren't for William O. Thorniley and a determined band of citizens who followed his lead, our Washington State ferries wouldn't bear the native American names that puzzle tourists (and a few natives as well).

It was early 1958 when the furor arose. Lloyd Nelson, a member of the State Toll Bridge Authority, had been given the innocent-sounding task of naming two new ferries in the state's seven-year-old expanded system. After reviewing the names of the most recent acquisitions—the *Rhododendron* and the *Olympic*, launched in 1953; the *Evergreen State*, christened in 1954—Nelson set sail with his imagination and came up with two sure winners: the *Vacation State* and the *Washington State*. A small item announcing the names appeared on a back page of the January 14, 1958, *Seattle Times*. With the pleased sensation of a job well done, Nelson went on to his next task.

He hadn't reckoned with William O. Thorniley. An employee of the Black Ball Ferry Line before the state acquired that private service in 1951, Thorniley had long advocated using native American names for the ferries. In fact, he had collected Chinook names for years and had personally named many of the ferries on the Black Ball Line. Now, when he heard the proposed names, Thorniley launched a campaign through the Seattle Chamber of Commerce to return to the tradition of native American ferry names. The result was a month-long controversy, with hundreds of citizens joining the fray.

State officials explained that native American names were too difficult for tourists to pronounce or understand—and the state intended to make the tourists as comfortable as possible. But to Bill Thorniley, a bored tourist was no more likely to return than a confused tourist. The redundant new names certainly bored him.

"*Vacation State!*" Thorniley snorted. "What's the matter with nice-sounding, colorful Indian names like *Bogachiel*, *Twana*, *Humptulips*, *Solduc*, *Dosewallips*, *Nooksack*, *Stillaguamish* and *Duckabush?*"

Poor Lloyd Nelson. Many Washingtonians agreed with Bill Thorniley, and there were plenty of ideas besides those he half-jokingly suggested. Letters poured into the State Toll Bridge Authority. Western Washington newspapers took up the hue and cry. Suggestions ranging from *Tahoma* (after the mountain) to *Squat* (Salish for silver salmon) and *Slob* (for chum salmon) were submitted by interested and irate citizens, complete with scorching comments about the state's lack of imagination.

Supporting a return to native American names, Edward E. Carlson, executive vice president of Western Hotels, asserted, "Anything that has to do with the romance of a region adds to its attraction for tourists. Look at the fantastic job they have done in Hawaii. We should lay emphasis on everything that's colorful and picturesque in the Puget Sound area."

Jack Gordon, publicity director for Greater Seattle, Inc., complained, "We've been trying too long to sell this to tourists with a picture of a totem pole and the Lake Washington Floating Bridge."

And Rudi Becker, connected with a harbor sightseeing service, branded the new names "unimaginative—just what you'd expect from politicians with no romance in their souls." In protest, Becker dubbed the 1918-model power dory he kept in his back yard the *Sales-Tax State*. (Now *there's* a name that would have stood the test of time.)

In the end, the state gave in. "All I want to do is smoke the peace pipe," Nelson declared. On February 15, just one month after the names *Vacation State* and *Washington State* had been announced, Nelson offered to withdraw them. Later, Thorniley served as the expert on Chinook Jargon when the state set up a nine-member committee for name selection. After three months, the committee decided on two new names: *Klahowya*, meaning "greetings" and *Tillikum*, meaning "friend."

Following are the native American names for some of the ferries currently in service. Most of the definitions were among Thorniley's papers and can be found, with other definitions, in *Ferry Boats*, a book by Mary Kline and George Bayless. (Thorniley had remarked that Chinook was exclusively a spoken language, so the accuracy of spelling and pronounciation in his list depended on the hearing and literacy of early settlers who first wrote them down.)

Elwha: The Elwha River on the northern Olympic Peninsula takes its name from the word for elk in the Clallam tongue.
Hiyu: Chinook Jargon for "plenty, much."
Hyak: Chinook Jargon for "fast, speedy."
Illahee: Chinook Jargon for "land, place" or "location."
Kaleetan: Chinook Jargon for "arrow."
Klahowya: Chinook Jargon for "greetings" or "welcome."
Klickitat: Native American tribe of south central Washington. Some early explorers claimed the word meant "beyond," but the majority seemed to favor "robbers" or "dog robbers."
Nisqually: Tribe which headquartered at the mouth of the Nisqually River.
Quinault: Lake Quinault and the Quinault tribe of the western Olympic Peninsula.
Spokane: Tribe in eastern Washington.
Tillikum: Chinook Jargon for "friend."
Walla Walla: Tribe in eastern Washington.

The most recent line of ferries was launched in the early 1980's, christened in the tradition of Northwest native American names.

Chelan: A lake on the eastern edge of the Cascade Mountain range, from the word for "deep water."
Issaquah: A city in western Washington, from a word of uncertain origin.

Kathlamet: Tribe in western Washington.
Kittitas: Shoal people; also defined as "land of bread."
Kitsap: Chief Kitsap, sub-chief of the Suquamish Tribe under Chief Sealth.
Sealth: Chief Sealth, after whom the city of Seattle was named. What's the best name for a ferry?

For a sense of regional history combined with a spirit of romance, Bill Thorniley's ideas were worth a few shots across the state's bow—and a second look. Take a ride on the *Sealth*, or the *Tillikum*, or someday (who knows?!) maybe even the *Duckabush*.

Margaret D. McGee, Seattle, WA

The Rambling Pram

On the car deck the lady parked the perambulator by the bicycle, braked the wheels, and departed upstairs. Three little girls approached reverently, attracted by the novelty of an old-fashioned baby carriage. They bent close to see what it contained. The biggest girl squatted to examine the wheels, pushed a lever, the pram moved slightly, and she pulled away.

Just then the ferry hooted and lurched. The girls ran to the front to see what was happening and the pram moved across the deck in a dignified manner. It paused beside a car, then jerked to life and sped across the rear deck to bang into the far railing where it changed course and rolled backwards toward the water.

Children, deckhands, and dogs gave chase. At the last second a hand grabbed the pram and drew it back aboard.

The owner appeared. "It's my grandmother's silver coffee service," she said. "This is the easiest way I've found over the years to transport it for her birthday party. Sometimes I wish it would throw itself overboard."

Reva Sparkes, Vashon Island, WA

Oh, Captain

The ferry boat was steaming,
    majestic, large and white,
when on the right or starboard
    Grindstone Harbor hove in sight.

Quoth the lady in the wheelhouse,
    old Cleo's child was she,
"Oh, Captain, bold Captain,
    please show my house to me."

The captain hesitated,
    and turned the wheel around.
Then with a mighty scrunching
    the *Elwha* went aground.

Now he sits beside the water,
    his voice sounds mournfully:
"A pox on all the women
    who have houses near the sea!"

Peggy Julian, Bainbridge Island, WA

Overslept

    The beep of a horn woke Betty. She pushed aside the blinds of her bedroom window. It was her carpool van. She had overslept! Her house was the last stop before the ferry so there wasn't a minute to spare.
    Stuffing her skirt, sweater, underclothes, shoes, stockings, and makeup into a bag, she threw on the longest coat she could find and dashed to the van.
    On board, Betty piled out of the car and ran across the deck to the stairwell. At the bottom step she collided with a deckhand, a man who worked that run every morning. Her bag flew open, scattering makeup and clothes. The deckhand helped her pick up the articles.
    A smile played on his face as he handed her a blue plaid skirt: "Are you wearing your nighty-night this morning, lady?"

Told to the Editor by Betty Gleason, Vashon Island, WA

9 to 5

The knot dissolves. I feel the
shudder of reverse engines.
People stir.
Cars
growl to life
in the depths of her belly.
A small line drops to the deck with
an oil-muffled snap—and I am home.

Paul Halvorson, Seattle, WA

November from the Ferryboat *Spokane*

Like candle wax
Seattle melts into Elliott Bay.
Highrises pour onto umbrellas,
streams of light
surrendering to gravity.
Pedestrians are unaware
the city is dissolving on their shoulders.

We leave the dock
and head into a black porridge
of rain, holding the blacker shores
we're going to
like nests behind our eyes. Soon
lights appear unslurred among the trees.
The island is intact.

Margi Berger, Bainbridge Island, WA

Muckelshoot Ferry
for William Garfield

Remember when we climbed the winter tree
and watched the black breath
of the Muckelshoot Ferry
boiling in the great pot of day?
You called her "River Singer"
and told me of the long darkness
brewing in her like thunder.

We'd walk the Quinault
to the old man of two souls
who told tales by sparrow,
by crow, by hawk; of white men
scattered dead along the river,
and their pale women,
bearers of black books,
kneeling to show their broken arms
and his indifference.

Words would drift in and out of him;
he'd speak of the ant,
the sharp edge of weeds,
fields of yellow flowers
running like butter
melting towards the sea.
He called the ferry "Devil"
and said its black breath
held nothing but curses.

Hannah Jones,
Bainbridge Island, WA

Fredrick Zydek, Omaha, NE

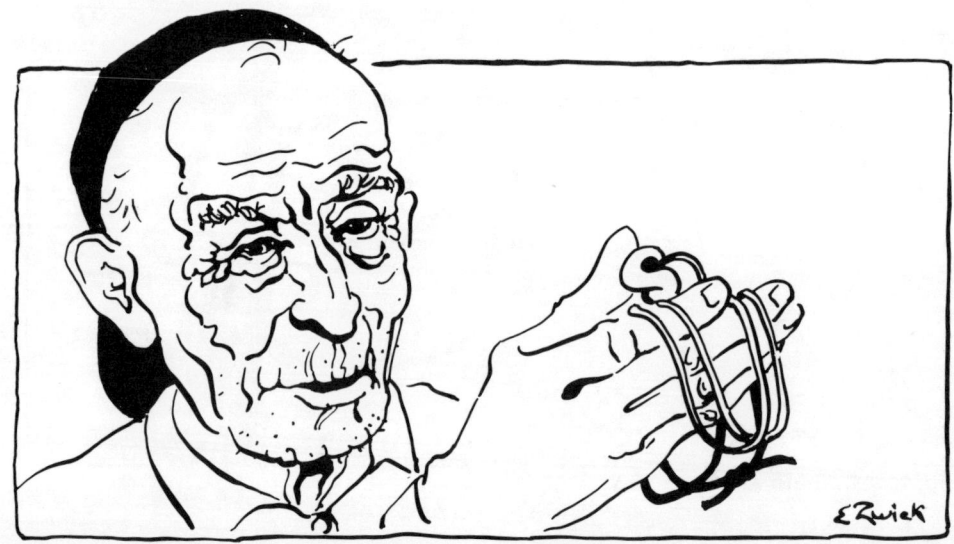
Elizabeth Zwick, Bainbridge Island, WA.

Night Ride to Orcas

The ferry *Klickitat* left the dock. The constant vibration of the engines changed slightly as we set off. This was the last ferry of the night and, since it was winter, the boat was abandoned except for me. I dozed, head propped against my pack on one of the green seats. I rode this run every Thursday night, after driving two hours from Olympia for a few days of rest on Orcas Island. I'd park my car at the landing, walk onto the ferry, then, when I got to Orcas, hitch a ride to a bit of land and a shack I owned.

The familiar motion of the boat had almost lulled me to sleep when I heard the jingle of keys, accompanied by a mop handle slapping against a metal pail. In the deserted ferry his voice was loud.

"So you're all settled down to hibernate, eh?"

I sat up, shoulders hunched, propped on my elbows. The old man, his face a baked apple with shiny seeds pressed deep into the eye sockets, hitched up his sagging green pants and put his free hand in his pocket. He toyed with the coins there as he looked off down the empty row of seats.

"I wish I were." Slowly I stretched my stiff neck.

"Yep. Well, I'll be all through in just a shake."

I nodded. Usually he winked at me, but tonight he merely grunted before shuffling off. Something about him seemed different. Inwardly I shrugged. He'd tell me if he wanted to.

I had ridden this ferry a long time. When I first met Henry, he'd formed an immediate attachment to me. After our first meeting (I had lifted my feet while he mopped under them), Henry, much to my surprise, had given me a sort of necklace he said he'd made himself—a thong threaded through a piece of old snail

32

shell. He bestowed this gift on me with the proclamation, "M'boy, I like you."

"I like you too," I had said, at a loss for words.

"Do an old man a favor and wear this—at least when you come up here and I'm around. You know, humor me." Then he gave me one of his tilt-of-the-head winks. So I wore the necklace each time I came up to Orcas. I gave him, in return, out of a sort of embarrassment, a wallet. From then on a bond existed between us—at least from Henry's point of view. Once the floors were mopped, the toilets unclogged, and the garbage cans emptied, Henry would come sit down across from me, take off his green and white baseball cap, pass his fingers a few times through what wisps of hair he might find on his skull, replace the cap (which he wore like a sort of yarmulke), get out his penknife, and begin to pare his nails. After a moment or two of pleasantries, he would tell me stories: some stories of Seattle when there was still sawdust in the streets, but mostly stories of the islands when they were still wild. Henry had ridden the ferries since the days when captains could navigate in a fog by the echoes of their ships' horns off the island shores. Often, tired as I was, I didn't pay attention to Henry's stories, but he didn't seem to mind. Mostly he seemed to forget I was even there and would go on in a sort of free association, while I nodded at intervals.

Some time after the ferry started, my half sleep was interrupted as Henry sat down, cup of coffee in hand. I waved weakly and wedged myself in the corner of my seat, against the window, to give at least a semblance of listening. The old man looked out the window, his hands, smelling faintly of ammonia, folded around his cup. The blue killer whale pictured there, caught in the midst of a tremendous vertical leap, seemed to be trying to escape Henry's grasp. When he spoke, his voice was low, in contrast to his usual raucous manner.

"Not a lot of folks tonight."

"I didn't see anyone else." He nodded, his lumpy face solemn. I yawned, trying to hide it with my hand, which I then used to prop up my head.

"Been a lean winter. Not a lot of people goin' 'cross."

My eyes were drooping. "Mm hm."

"It'll pick up by summer. But that's a long ways aways."

"Sure is."

Henry looked down into his cup, the surface of the coffee agitated by the motion of the boat. I suppressed another yawn. I waited. By this time he had usually begun one of his tales. His head bowed slightly. He could even be praying. In this position, he might have been at confession. A fine confessor I would make. Just as my head was about to slide from my hand to the table, he began, his voice even softer, never looking up from his cup, so I had to strain to hear.

"They say there is something . . . something in the islands, that no man has ever really seen—completely. All at once."

Ah, a ghost story. Bigfoot perhaps. I settled myself as comfortably as the impossible seat allowed.

". . . something not really alive . . . made up of bits of bone showing through patches of hide and hair, like a carcass of a deer you come upon in the woods, and also moss and lichen and fungus, but with streamers of kelp, some say, draped over it, and barnacles crusted in spots. And the smell! Like the lowest tide on the hottest day, when things that shouldn't be exposed are—and they rot and a stench rises from the ground like, like, nothing you've ever smelled. Or would want to. The Indians, they called it" (he hesitated a long moment) "I forget what they called it."

Here, I believe, I fell asleep. I caught myself, repeatedly, then dropped off again, hearing only snatches of the story.

". . . tracks sometimes like a deer, but bigger, or just none at all but a fragment of odd bone or strand of sea grass, but miles from the water . . . how to say it? A provider of sorts I guess. I provide, make sure there is a steady supply of . . . um . . . protected you. Because I liked you, you see . . . like the Hebrews. In ancient times—times of the Bible—Moses said, I think, put an X on your door, and your first born won't be killed like the Egyptians; would be passed over by the plague. But if there was no mark, then, even if the family was Hebrew, the hand . . . Now I don't claim to be no Moses . . . another man might ask forgiveness. Not me. I've lived long enough, seen enough that . . . tell you this, because you . . . I don't know. Kept to myself all this time . . . man just needs to talk. You know? But there it is, and that's it. Some reason I thought I could tell you. That's all there is."

I had, over the past few months, developed a talent for waking up and looking intently at Henry just as he finished. It gave, I thought, the impression that I had been hanging onto his every word. I used this talent now and, clearing my throat a little, I spoke.

"I'm sure that's not all. You'll remember something else, I bet. You know, Henry, I've been thinking. You really should write some of this down. It's invaluable, your experience."

Henry looked up from his coffee, still untouched. For the first time that night, he looked me straight in the eye. He drew his breath sharply, as if to say something, then released it, allowing his frame to sag. He said nothing more. Immediately I knew I had said something foolish, and struggled for some way to repair the damage. But just then the Purser announced our arrival at Orcas. I turned to Henry but he was once again staring into his cup. I opened my mouth to say something, but thought better of it. Taking up my pack, I reached over and gave him a pat on the shoulder. He nodded distractedly. Stung, I turned away and descended to the lower levels.

Once off the ferry and on the road, walking among the trees and looking over my shoulder periodically for a pair of headlights to round the bend behind me, I began to go over what it might have been that I'd missed. Tonight's story had seemed important to the old man. What had he been saying? Suddenly I stopped short. On this trip I'd forgotten to wear the necklace he'd given me. I shook my head and sighed.

A breeze blew in my face. I raised my head, feeling the breeze move through my hair. I coughed. Something putrid was in the air. The tide must be low. I looked around. The trees and the darkness they harbored seemed to be crowding me, to be reaching out. "... like low tide ..." he had said. But this was dead Winter. No low tides. And the wind was in my face, while the water was at my back. My chest felt constricted, as it had once when I'd seen a pig butchered. I had to force myself to breathe. Something in the brush moved. I spoke out loud, the last two words sing-song:
"I don't like this ..."
Instantly I regretted having spoken.

Eric Perret, Seattle, WA

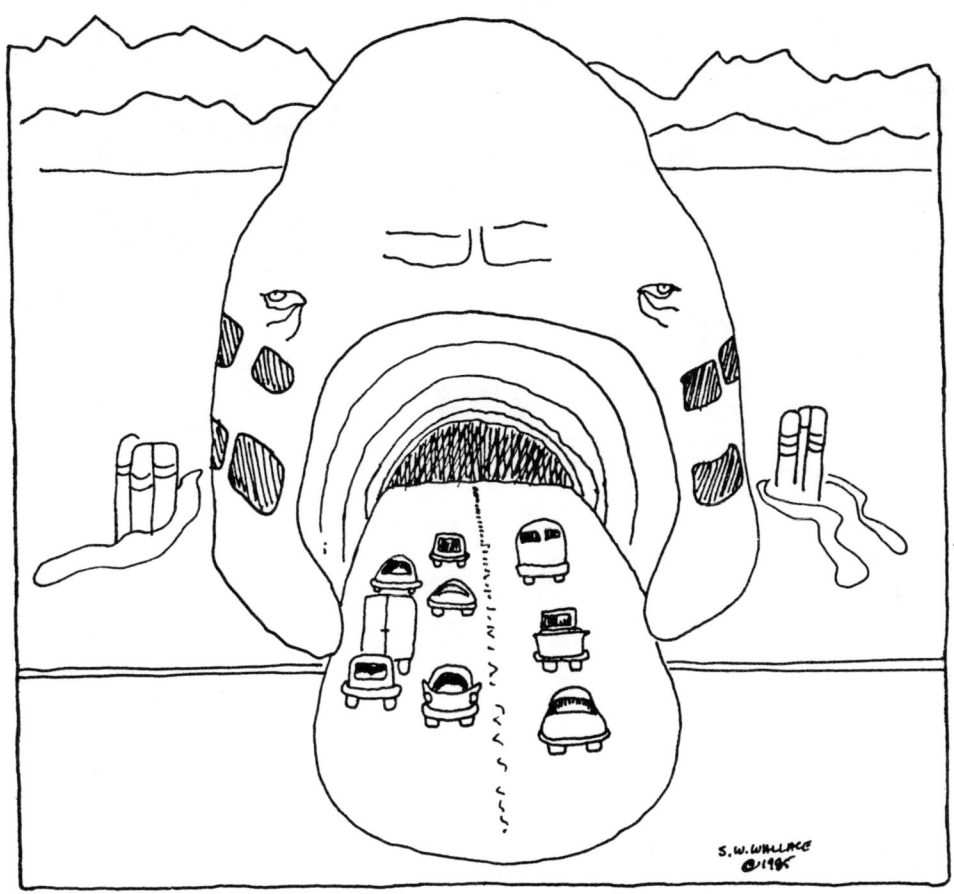

Susan Wallace, Bainbridge Island, WA

Slithering Silvers!

On one of the initial runs of the steel-electrics when returning from Sidney to Friday Harbor, the ferry responded to a purse-seiner's call for assistance. The fishboat whistled the ferry down, came alongside, and explained that a bad leak was filling up the fish hold, a flood of water seemed to be coming in from the stern-tube. The crew of eight were prepared to abandon the boat with the freeboard getting less and less and the water not draining to the bilge pump.

The seiner captain asked if the ferry could stand by for a while in the event their boat sank before they could plug the leak. He said in the meantime they would throw out the salmon to lighten the boat and try to get at the trouble. They had only the haul from one set aboard, probably 500 fish, so it wouldn't take long. The boat had two fish pews (poles with a curved prong) and they would pitch the salmon from the after end of the hold up to the open deck of the ferry. The ferry captain on the upper deck responded with, "Have at it, we'll wait."

The boat eased alongside the end of the ferry, made fast, and the salmon began to fly aboard. In fifteen minutes the after deck was covered with slithering "silvers" and the fishermen were able to pull out the floor section of the hold and get at the leak. They found the packing almost gone from around the bearing and by dint of fast but wet work, they tightened the gland enough for them to feel safe and yell up to the captain that they would be okay to poke along to Friday Harbor. The captain quickly pointed to the fish on the deck, then to the fish hold—about 200 had been tossed over. The seiner's captain pointed back and yelled, "The fish are all yours for the help and the stand-by!" Then as the seiner drifted astern, the passengers shouted, "Good fishing to you!"

Everybody on board went home with a salmon, compliments of the Washington State Ferries and the crew of the seiner *Golden Light.*

Excerpt from Ferry Story *by Mike Skalley, Seattle, WA*

Line-up

Cars trickled through the three ticket gates for a position on the already overloaded dock. The ferry pulled out, leaving a row of cars to wait for the next departure. I pulled in at the end of the line, leaving a few feet of space in front of my car. Suddenly I heard a noise and felt my car move forward a few inches. Bump! Bump! Bump! I whirled around in my seat. A woman in the car behind me was pushing my car forward with short bursts of acceleration. I saw the set look on her face and shrugged. When she had closed the gap, I signaled her to stop. She returned my signal and settled back in her seat with a satisfied grin.

Richard Braden, Bainbridge Island, WA

Knute Berger, Bainbridge Island, WA

Speedy

Five minutes after boarding the ferry at Horseshoe Bay in Vancouver, B.C., passengers were settled back into their seats, reading their papers or closing their eyes for a nap. Suddenly a loudspeaker announced, via a recorded message, that the ship would be arriving at Departure Bay in Nanaimo in ten minutes. Passengers sat up, their mouths open wide. Young people rushed to the deck to check the landscape.

"What's that?" an old gentleman's querulous voice could be heard above the hubbub. "It takes an hour and a half to reach Departure Bay!"

The loudspeaker came on again, this time an unrecorded voice: "We're fast, but not that fast."

Somehow the recorded message had been flipped on by mistake.

Told to the Editor by Captain Zak Farid, Nanaimo, B.C.

A Ferry Affair

Grey clouds churned. The wind blew fast. Waves splashed against the dock.
The ferry waited patiently. The hour was five o'clock.

A crowd of tired commuters rushed to board the evening boat.
Motors muttered; engines hummed. The cars were soon afloat.

Riders all raced up the stairs, a window seat to find.
"Warf, woof, woof," the whistle wailed. The city fell behind.

Passengers laughed, ate and drank. Everyone was merry.
Everyone, that is, except sad and lonely Kari.

Kari'd lost her job that day. She ripped her favorite skirt.
She hadn't eaten anything. Her lunch dropped in the dirt.

"Is this seat taken?" someone asked. Her blue eyes rose to look.
Wavy hair and handsome face. One glance was all it took.

Her heart went thump. Her breath came fast. He was the ideal man.
But her messy hair! Her tattered skirt! Just then her stocking ran.

"Looks like a storm," he said and took the spot beside her.
He smiled. "My name is Harry." She wished someone would guide her.

Rain streaked the window; lightning flashed. Like cannons boomed the thunder.
Kari's eyes searched round the space for something to hide under.

"Don't be afraid," he comforted. "The ferry's safe and sound."
Then suddenly came a monstrous bang. The ferry ran aground.

Kari fell right in his lap. It was so nice and cozy.
"You've torn your skirt!" he said. She felt her cheeks grow rosy.

The captain came and told them they'd be home by and by.
He couldn't move the ferry until the tide was high.

She had six hours only. Time enough to charm him?
She musn't overdo. She feared she might alarm him.

Harry gazed at Kari and she gazed back at him.
She didn't look so bad, now that the lights were dim.

"This will be fun!" he laughed and took her hand, did Harry.
"You are the girl with whom I wish to tarry on the ferry."

She flirted through the evening. Her purpose never varied.
When the tide had turned, she knew that soon she would be married.

The big day came. The guests arrived. Good friends from near and far.
In rustling silks and dark wool suits, they came by truck and car.

They came aboard the ferry. This was a special ride.
The captain spoke. Rings were exchanged. The bride's mother cried.

Beneath "THEY'VE WED," the newspaper, with headlines bold and blarey,
announced the joyous news: "HARRY, KARI ON THE FERRY."

Janet Lonergan, Bellevue, WA

J.L.

Issy

The *Issaquah* was the first of six ferries recently built for the Washington State Ferry System. As soon as it was launched one problem after another developed. The breakdowns created much controversy and the ferry was frequently taken out of service.

As might be expected, graffiti became common. On the inside walls of the women's restroom were scribbled these lines:

"Now that you've sat down with time to think,
Pray the Lord that Issy won't sink."

Told to the Editor by Asta Schade (age 85), Vashon Island, WA

You're the One Who's Worried

Getting to the ferry on time is no problem for me. Getting there with my husband is another matter.

One Sunday afternoon when we had to go to Seattle I started fidgeting at 1:00. "Bill, which ferry should we catch?"

"I don't know. I'll look at the schedule in a few minutes."

"Look now. You've been reading for two hours."

"You look. You're the one who's worried."

We decided on the 2:30 ferry.

I started toward the kitchen. An hour and a half wasn't much time. There was my shower, my nails, the dog to feed, the dishwasher to fill.

"Bill, the timer is set for 2:00. We ought to leave here at 2:20. Okay?" (We live three minutes away from the dock.)

His newspapers rustled and a groan emanated from behind them.

I shrugged and retreated to my bedroom. At 2:00 I had on my freshly polished white shoes and wore a pale blue dress with matching scarf.

The timer went off. The newspaper tent that hid my husband fell to the floor and Bill came blasting out of the recliner like a hydroplane. "My God, I forgot to water the roses," he said as he rushed out the door. "Do you know where my green knit shirt is? Throw it in the wash for me, will you, Hon?"

My blood pressure rose. I stalked to the dirty clothes closet, found the shirt, gave it a quick rinsing and flung it in the dryer. I gathered my nail-polishing things and went to the living room, as far away from where he was dressing as possible. Each time the door slammed or a drawer shut hard, my body flinched.

At 2:15 Bill dashed out of his room and yelled, "Change the hose, will you, Joyce?"

"Sorry," I answered, sugary sweet, through clenched teeth. "It would ruin my white shoes."

"Take your shoes off!"

He stormed through the room, zipping up his fly, his shoes untied. He pushed back the sliding glass door and loped out into the yard.

Making sure to hold my fingers so the coat of polish wouldn't smear, I gathered my purse and Kleenex and started out the front door, calling back to him, "I'll wait in the car."

Nine minutes I fumed. He had done it again. I honked the horn.

At two-twenty-six and a half, he locked the house and hurried to the car, his face businesslike and his eyes going every direction except toward me. He started the motor and hurtled the car out of the driveway.

"There'll be a line-up. We won't get on." I grabbed the overhead strap.

No answer.

The Toyota strained its motor as we whizzed along the road and raced down Parking Lot Hill in record time. When we reached the dock, all cars were loaded and the deckhands headed down the ramp. I bit my nails and boiled. Bill relaxed with a beatific smile.

One deckhand turned and motioned us on. The rest of the crew stood with car blocks in hand and chains ready to hook together. The Toyota skidded into the last available place.

"I'll kill him," I swore as I collapsed against the backrest.

Joyce Delbridge, Vashon Island, WA

The 50-yard dash off the car deck.

Susan Wallace, Bainbridge Island, WA

A Very Special Problem

Ferries of the steel/electric class tend to build up pressure in the toilets overnight, causing a spray of water to shoot up over the level of the toilet seats. It is the watchman's responsibility to flush each toilet in the morning before passengers board.

One day on the *Illahee* we had a new watchman. No one thought to tell her about this important responsibility.

On the first run I noticed a dignified, well dressed older lady entering the restroom. After a while I heard the toilet flush, followed by a high-pitched scream.

A few minutes later the distraught woman stood outside my office. She was so rattled she couldn't communicate. I apologized and tried to explain. I doubt if she heard a word I said. Finally she stalked away, muttering to herself.

This incident served as a reminder to all of us to keep the watchman alerted about this duty.

Robert D. Johnson, Clallam Bay, WA

Shiners

In the summer of 1929, my mother and I came back to Seattle from Alaska. Mother had been teaching school in the native village of Klukwan, and now we were invited to visit her sister, my Aunt Florence, in the Fauntleroy area.

Aunt Florence had three sons, all older than I. I was nine at the time, and these cousins were old enough "to think about girls," which left me out. I'd rather play ball any old day. Because of this difference, and because I was the new kid, I had no friends. If I wanted amusement, I had to make it.

The ferry to Vashon Island docked within sight of Aunt Florence's house. It was smaller than the super-class ferries of today, but it looked large to me. When I heard its whistle, I would run to the dock to watch the passengers come and go. I loved boats, and to me the Vashon ferry was as thrilling as the ocean-going vessels we rode to Alaska.

One day it struck me. Why not take a trip to Vashon Island? The fare wasn't much—I forget just what it was—25 cents one way, maybe—and it would give me something to do besides playing a lonely game of mumblety-peg on Aunt Florence's lawn. Perhaps because she was eager to get me out of her hair for a few hours, my mother gave me passage and lunch money and sent me on my way.

I took an early morning ferry. As soon as I boarded, I rushed up the stairs, through the place where all the passengers sit, and onto the outside deck. There I looked down on the deckhands as they loaded cars and farm trucks. After we pulled out, I was all over the ship from bow to stern, topside to keel. Well, I couldn't get to the keel, but I did manage to see the huge engines in the engine room. When the ferry slowed, I raced to the outside deck, this time at the opposite end of the ferry, and watched the Vashon dock grow bigger and bigger.

As soon as we docked at Vashon, I checked the schedule for my return trip. First, though, I'd explore Vashon.

It didn't seem to me there was much to explore. Vashon was a small village some five miles away at the center of the island. The few buildings huddled nearby took only a few minutes to see.

I returned to the dock to await my ferry. There was a bunch of boys on the dock, fishing through the cracks for shiners, which were flat fish four or five inches long. The shiners got their name from the way they flashed in the dark green water under the dock where they gathered for feeding. When a boy caught a shiner, he pulled the wriggling critter up through a crack between the boards of the dock. The cracks were about an inch wide, just wide enough to slip the fish through by turning it until the flat side fit the crack.

This little game fascinated me. I decided to try my luck. I spent my lunch money on a hook and line which I bought from a boy who had an extra supply. After I caught the hang of turning the fish to fit the crack, I snagged several shiners in no time at all. They were voracious little fish that would bite on anything from snips of bacon to bits of brethren shiners.

I was hooked. Whenever my mother could spare the cash, I sailed to Vashon Island for a day of fishing. Women came down to the dock and bought our shiners, so we made a few pennies besides enjoying the sport.

I never took the fish home. My Aunt Florence didn't want them. If I hadn't peddled mine, I usually gave them to the boy who sold me my hook and line. He would nod in a matter-of-fact way and store them in his wooden fishbox.

Along with the shiners there was another fish, a red, thick-bodied cod. It could have been related to a red snapper, but I'm not sure. Sometimes they would bite, but they were too big to squeeze through an inch crack. The women shoppers were especially eager for these cod, and would pay 25 or 30 cents for one, if the fisherman could land it.

The only way to land one was by working it over to the edge of the dock. If the fisherman got that far without losing the fish, he'd swing it out and another boy would make a grab for it. Sometimes we had a hand net. Then the cod was easily captured. If no net was around, there were some pretty desperate capers to land that fish. Often as not, the cod broke free and swam off, the luckless fisherman gazing sadly after the fish as it disappeared into deep water.

I never caught a red cod but I did catch my share of shiners. And I had many a wonderful ride on the ferry, smelling the sea, vowing someday to skipper some kind of vessel myself. I never did, but I have a fine memory of that summer.

Robert H. Redding, Sequim, WA

Judith Lawrence, Vashon Island, WA

The Mating of the *Hyak*

Hyak passes, a blue dress
dropped about her ankles.
Yakima laughs to himself
and casually asks her
when she gets off work.

No one even notices this meeting.
Nobody that is except the island.
Blake Island. Green as green is
sees it every time it happens.
Blake now has another minute's gossip.

They will be gone but also
they'll be back.
The island knows the island
always watches. Watches
as they dance and glide
in a cold blue embrace.

Blake acknowledges the cold white moon
laughing in the afternoon.

We put our smokes out
you glance at your watch
as I sip my lukewarm coffee.
I say, "Rainier is out today."
You say, "Yes, it's lovely.
          Let's go down."

How could we ever be suspicious?
We are just passengers and they
are just boats. How many years
has this been going on?

Hal B. Fernandez, Federal Way, WA

Cartwheeling

across the top deck of the ferry
I watch the Cheshire moon grin
frown, then grin again.

My fingers spread across
the coarse deck,
then arms stretch up to the swirling sky.

City lights swim
in waves above
while my tennies swoop through the stars.

Kris Hutchison, Bainbridge Island, WA

Walla Walla at Night

The sky
chocolate cake layered with dark clouds
is reflected in the deck
coated with water like cellophane on cards.
Raindrops leapfrog down the windows
of the covered observation deck.

The couple sits
under the heat lamp
knees fitted together like jigsaw puzzle pieces.
Sitting next to them
I don't really exist
being just a deck fixture
like the telescope.

That other night
in the summer
we touched lightly
in the shadowed corner
behind the smokestack;
you absorbed the cold with your back
and I left warm prints on your skin
with my hands.

Sara Rekow, Bainbridge Island, WA

The Ferry That Will Live Forever

May 10, 1930
"Wow!"

The ribbon-wrapped bottle exploded against the ferry *Vashon's* bow with a mighty spray. High school girls, I among them, bunched near the sponsor's platform and peered at the 17 feet of hull looming above us.

"She sure practiced her swing." Our classmate Mary Berry who had just christened the *Vashon* had struck the bow like a baseball pro.

"She splashed champagne on her new orchid suit!"

"That's not champagne. It's Puget Sound water." True. The Eighteenth Amendment to the United States Constitution made no exceptions for boat launchings.

The contest to select Miss Vashon to launch the vessel had been fiercely fought on Vashon Island. Residents could cast as many votes as they wished, at a penny a vote. Ignoring the Depression, the town of Dockton had poured votes into the polling places five hundred at a time.

"Those fishermen have gone crazy," we said. "Five dollars is two day's pay, just about."

"They don't care as long as Mary wins."

Mary Berry had coasted to a win in a veritable pennyslide.

Everyone rallied around our queen. When the steamboat *Winslow* called at Vashon Heights to take us to the ceremony, we left the island temporarily depopulated. Five hundred spectators, the largest crowd ever to attend a launching at the Lake Washington Shipyards, watched the *Vashon* slide down the ways.

"She didn't stick halfway down."

". . . Or capsize."

Done with the launching, we attended to other matters, mainly straightening the seams of our silk stockings; the boys polished their oxfords on their corduroy pantlegs. Guests who had come by automobile departed in a procession: Model A Fords, Chevy touring cars, and an occasional stately Pierce-Arrow. Moving with the crowd reboarding the *Winslow*, we began the pairing-up game for the ride home with the boys.

Few spectators realized they had been present at a significant moment in Puget Sound history. Contracts to build the *Vashon* had been signed January 30, 1930. A two-ended boat built of Northwest Douglas fir, she had a specially designed eight-cylinder Estep engine with a clutch at each end to activate whichever propeller was required. On May 29 she went for her only trial run. The machinery ran like a fine watch.

That afternoon the largest Puget Sound ferry, with a 90-car capacity, began her career on the Fauntleroy-Vashon-Harper run. For 50 years she would help form the vital water highways that linked Sound islanders and the Olympic Peninsula to the mainland. She would help make possible the growth of industry and

M.S. Vashon   1930-1936   Kitsap County Transportation Co.
White hull and superstructure, dark red trim, black stack

M.S. Vashon   1936-1951   Puget Sound Navigation Co., Black Ball Line
Black hull, white superstructure, buff trim, red and black stack

M.V. Vashon   1951-1981   Washington State Ferries
Dark green hull, white superstructure, green trim and stack

Darsie Beck, Vashon Island, WA

population in communities isolated by water.

But change caught up with the *Vashon*. By 1941, cars were longer, and her capacity was reduced to 60 vehicles. New superferries, that borrowed her efficient clutch design and incorporated her V-shaped hull, took over the south Sound routes. She moved to the San Juan Islands where she earned the nickname "Old Reliable."

By 1979 the *Vashon* was the fleet's last all-wood ferry, the only vessel without hydraulic or electric steering. The huge wheel, an "arm-buster," had to be turned manually. In strong currents or a blow she required two men to keep the bucking wheel from spinning out of control. Now the smallest and slowest ferry, she carried only 35 cars. Infected with dry rot, she was too expensive to recondition. The *Vashon* was ready to retire.

She received listing on the National Register of Historic Places. Old Reliable's friends proposed many ideas for her use: turn her into a terminal building, a floating classroom, a hotel and lounge, a museum, a library, or make her the state's pavilion at the Expo 86 celebration in Vancouver, B.C.

Put up for auction, she had no bidders. A marina refused moorage because she "might sink." Thereafter she squatted on the Seattle waterfront, paint peeling, a rotting derelict, an embarrassment.

March 10, 1985

I greeted the *Vashon* at Pier 70. We were two old ladies meeting again after 55 years. The car deck held a strange conglomeration: ladders, cans of paint, lumber—evidences of the *Vashon's* reconditioning; stacks of mattresses waiting to be put in place—promises of what the *Vashon* would become. I joined a handful of guests on the passenger deck where her recommissioning would take place.

When the champagne bottle exploded on the rail, the United States flag snapped smartly in the breeze, and the old ferry's whistle sent gulls wheeling into the gray sky. The *Vashon/Seattle International Hostel* had been christened.

This time I stood near enough to be spattered with champagne. "Is it real?" someone asked, looking at the bottle. "Oh, it's an expensive brand."

Captain Ray Armistead, her new owner, smiled. "The old girl deserves it." He referred to the *Vashon*, not me.

He was delighted with his floating hostel. Refurbished and powered by her still-magnificent engine, she would be moored on the Seattle waterfront. Occasionally she would visit other Puget Sound cities, and each August move into Lake Washington to cleanse her keel in fresh water.

During the vessel's first summer as hostel, she briefly went on sale once more.

"Same old story. Nobody'll give her moorage," scoffed one disbeliever. "All that sweat and money spent on the old lady. Wasted."

"The *Vashon's* future has been threatened before." I recalled how Old Reliable had earned her name—fighting the treacherous tides and squalls in the Strait of Juan de Fuca. "Her owner is a fighting man. They'll make it."

The *Vashon*, her moorage problem solved at the last moment, now anchors in friendly West Seattle waters awaiting her turn in drydock for reconditioning of her hull. She still rises and falls with the tides, ready to rock the cradles of adventurers, young and old, who are traveling "on a dime." Ferry buffs who love the sights, sounds, and smells of old boats are sure to find her—and perhaps some children curious to see how things used to be.

Her troubles are not ended, but the *Vashon* may yet live forever.

Kathryn E. White, Seattle, WA

Elegy for the *Vashon*

She dreams speed
but wakes
to soft knots and rust—the black worms
of fifty years coiling night
inside her beams. She
hears disgrace
in the slow groans
of each nail clawed free.

Down the Sound's throat
from Anacortes
she came,
Queen of the San Juans,
ceaseless pumps keeping her trim.
Heavy lines tied up
a small legend
to a cold slip in Eagle Harbor,
cold-shouldered by the fleet master's daughters,
an old lady blinded by steel.

Chetzemoka took burial
at sea while under tow—water to water.
Salt is merciless, we already knew,
but men are worse.

This beloved *Vashon*,
with the faithful hold
of her engine room
split open—
the lions of sunlight
inside, loose and roaring.

Tom Snyder, Indianola, WA

Crossing Water

In the passage from Edmonds to Kingston
we stand on the lee side
of the weather deck
our women in the sun
bright blue
brisk breeze
over the silver Sound

Then just hours
after a walk over old forts
mortar batteries and brick
lunch
an afternoon coffee in Poulsbo
nothing said
everything changes
no anger or loud words
rather a flotsam of gestures

In the passage from Winslow to Seattle
we stand windward
all four of us in the frail sun
the diesel fumes
those tall buildings
the silent mountains
an Asian freighter
Singapore   Hong Kong   Manila

Somewhere in the crossing of the years
while we passed forty
you passed too near that certain island
smelled the gray
saw too far into the pit
where something touched you
for we acknowledge now
a new silence
sure as iron bulkheads

At a point in time
we will dock
descend the ladderway
step from the boat
never to cross these waters together again

David B. McCreary, Seattle, WA

The Boy Who Wandered Around

Seven-year-old Mark Bowden had a tendency to wander around on family trips. The Seattle boy was wandering around the ferry *Walla Walla* on a return trip from Bainbridge Island one Sunday in June when he found a black leather case under a cafeteria table. Mark's mother Ann assumed the black case held a camera or traveling gear and told her son to take it to the cafeteria cashier.

A few minutes later the family was paged and told to report to the first mate's office. There, the man who had lost the case thanked the boy and pulled out his money clip.

Ann thought, "Oh, that's nice, he's going to give him a dollar." But the man moved his dollar bills aside and handed Mark a $100 bill. Ann couldn't believe it—she thought the man didn't realize what he was doing. She said that was too much money. They argued over it and he finally said, "Look, you have no idea how much money you've saved me."

It was only later, after the grateful man left without identifying himself, that ferry workers told the Bowdens exactly how much money had been in the case: $11,000.

Mark, who was entering the second grade at John Hay Elementary School on Queen Anne, said that he planned to put the money in the bank and save it for something he really wanted.

From an article in the Seattle Post-Intelligencer
Kerry Godes, Reporter, Seattle, WA

Jean Iverson

The Storm

"George, do you think we can make it to Wesley Gardens tonight?" I yelled in his ear.

The howl of the wind lashing the Whidbey Island ferry dock nearly swept away his answer, but his lips moved in assent. George Cole was resting his ninety-year-old head against the back of the car seat, his eyes closed. He was a devout man—a lay minister. Was he praying? Or was he near exhaustion? In the eerie late evening light his face looked pale.

Earlier that night George had been the speaker for a conference on creativity at Camp Casey on southwest Whidbey. He'd delivered a rousing talk about his boyhood years on a Kansas farm. Now it was my responsibility to drive him home to Des Moines, south of Seattle.

Together we watched the bobbing lights of the approaching ferry as the captain struggled to dock her between the rows of creaking pilings.

At the ticket booth we overheard the agent talking with a customer: "High tide . . . record wind velocity . . . ferries closing down . . . last crossings."

We teeter-tottered across the hinged ramp onto the tossing ship. The chains rattled as they were secured just behind my rear bumper. "The last of the last," I said. Deck hands scurried to kick chocks under our wheels. That would have given us comfort if it hadn't been for their warning: "Set your brakes and stay in your car."

The signal bell and whistle rang and tooted like Christmas toys as we plunged out of the slip toward Mukilteo.

The storm was a word processor spelling green across a seascape screen. The ferry now and then corrected itself at the command of the master, and read back edited lines in creaks and groans.

My white hands gripped the tiller of my car as I helped pilot the ferry. Up sideways on the crests. Slam down in the troughs. My stomach floated somewhere between the left front visor and the rear view mirror. I summoned a brave, reassuring smile for George. He gave a little chuckle and said, "You're scared, aren't you?"

Without pause, he launched into his performance of the evening. His timing was uncanny. The ferry and the tempest provided sound effects: "I had a buddy who fought at Verdun. He was plenty scared, too." Commuters became doughboys shivering in trenches. Dark shapes of cars were caissons, trucks, tanks. The boat's engines rumbled defiance to the enemy seas. Belly down, it crept forward. I was transported—above and remote from the storm.

Suddenly, all forward motion of the ferry was suspended, punctuated by a sickening drop and thud. Then a rushing growl like the approach of a tidal bore. A gigantic wave smashed over the bow and a wall of water thundered the length of the ferry, carrying scores of wheel chocks that thumped against hubcaps and disappeared over the stern into the churning wake. This story was alive.

The Mukilteo landing lights and lighthouse flashed by. We had missed the dock.

The captain tried again. Bells signaled wildly for reverse—then full speed ahead.

Mentally we pulled together, two backseat captains. Another failure to dock. A third time we approached, this time from far up the channel with the tide ploughing us into the open wings of the slip. We shuddered to a stop amid clangings and shouts from the deckhands. I collapsed into the curve of my backrest and released my grip from the steering wheel. The usual twenty-minute crossing had taken well over an hour.

"That was a corker!" George admitted as we threaded our way toward Des Moines through downed signs and fallen trees. "But if I had drowned in that storm, I'd have felt satisfied with my life." He crinkled into a beatific glow. "You needn't have worried about me."

Jean Isabelle Iverson, Seattle, WA

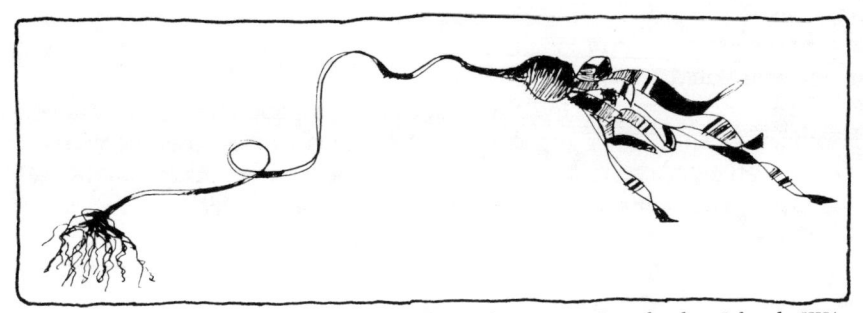

Greg Onewein, Bainbridge Island, WA

Toot, Toot, Toot, Toot, Toot

One Sunday, a ferry left Southworth dock, heading across West Passage to Vashon Island. A large yacht barreled down the passage from the North. The captain whistled for a port-to-port passing but there was no response. Then he tried the radio. Still no response.

Finally he blew toot-toot-toot-toot-toot, the danger signal. Still the yacht kept coming at a fast clip. The captain backed down and brought the ferry to a stop. By the time the ship responded, it was so close to the yacht the captain could see the pilot at the pleasure craft's wheel. A young boy about nine years old gripped the wheel with one hand and waved gaily to the deckhands at the ferry railing.

The yacht had traveled south about two minutes longer when suddenly an adult voice blared over the radio. "Shorry, shipper. I didn't she your vessel or hear your whishle."

Captain Glen Willers, Vashon Island, WA

Stress! Does it Ride With You?

As a ferry commuter, is stress a part of your personal crew? Do you carry your worries aboard? To a degree everyone does, but there are also occurences on the ferry that trigger annoyance and contribute to an increased level of stress.

For example, I asked commuters what bugged them the most while riding the ferry. We'll refrain from printing the comments that went along with their responses in order to preserve the innocence of children. But here are the most common "bugs":

People clipping their fingernails
Smoking in the non-smoking areas
People combing their hair
People leaving trash, crumbs, garbage
Loud radio playing
Raucous video games
Loud conversations and laughing

I'm sure you could add these to the list:

People who eat bananas and throw the skins at people in the adjoining seats
Teenagers making out right in front of your eyes (stress, hell—envy!)

So what can people do to overcome the stress these create? As my psychotherapist friend David Mitchell says, "To counteract a stressful situation, do something." Don't just sit there and stew. Concentrate on something to take the annoyance off your mind. Balance your checkbook. "It's a nice tidy package and you feel good when it's all wrapped up."

Here are other suggestions commuters may relate to.

Maintain a sense of control over your environment. Get to the terminal early. Leave home early enough to avoid traffic and pick your own parking space. If someone else's car is in the space you like, tie a barrel to their bumper and leave.

Ask people who are playing their radio too loudly to turn it down. If they refuse, use the means provided by our lawmakers. Keep a good old patriotic firecracker in your purse. When the radio listener isn't looking, slip the lighted firecracker into the battery compartment.

I tried this approach once. After the explosion, the offender sat there ecstatically holding the wreckage and said, "Boy, what a number!"

Try meditating. Here are some suggestions to make it work. Get into a comfortable position. Close your eyes. Concentrate on a single word or phrase like "Walla Walla" or "Puget Sound." Cast off all other thoughts. But be sure to leave a wake-up call. Several meditators have crossed the Sound three times before a crew person woke them up.

Try exercising. Here are some easy ones to repeat. Walk around the ferry. Open your fists and close them tightly. Massage your neck. Open your eyes and close them in a tight squint. But don't overdo. A friend of mine got a mental hernia squinting too hard. Another unsuspecting exerciser was given mouth to mouth resuscitation by a passing medic.

Probably some excellent serious advice comes from Jennifer James, therapist, whose column appears in the Sunday *Seattle Times/Seattle Post Intelligencer*. Recently she said, "Perhaps the most important survival tool, besides a clear set of values, is a sense of humor."

Also, don't forget the ultimate advantage of being a commuter. You can take any ferry you want. Just for the heck of it take a late one—say an 8:30 a.m. When you get to the office tell your boss you're late because the ferry went aground. Just think, you'll be the center of attention twice. Once, for about five minutes while everyone listens as you tell the story. And then when your boss watches the evening news and doesn't see a thing about a ferry going aground.

And finally, heed the words of my dearest grandmother who always counseled that regularity reduces stress. Catch the same ferry every day and drink plenty of prune juice.

Reprinted from an article in the Enetai
by Steele Coddington, Bainbridge Island, WA

A Proper Banker

Beulah Reed started worrying as it came close to the ferry's 8 a.m. departure time from Tahlequah. Her son-in-law, Bill Mish, had a new job as a bank official in Tacoma. He had to catch this boat to get to work on time. Where was he? He was always so reliable. Car trouble?

No. There he was, sprinting down the dock in his pajamas and robe! His pants, shirt, coat, and tie streamed from his arms as he skimmed past the gate at the last second.

He raced up the stairway, and with a sheepish grin toward Beulah, headed for the men's room. Ten minutes later, as the engines slowed for docking, he emerged fully dressed, looking like a proper banker, his p.j.s and robe in a neat bundle under his arm. "Overslept," he explained to his mother-in-law.

"Glad you made it," she said. "You look fine."

"Thanks! But I'll have to use the stapler. I forgot my tie clasp—and my wallet. Could I borrow a buck for lunch?"

Told to the Editor by Bill Mish, Vashon Island, WA

Michael DeVoe, Vashon Island, WA

Quinault George

George was a large gull, with flesh-colored legs, white head and tail, pearl gray wings tipped with black, and a spot of gray above his beady eyes.

He looked over the possibilities for freeloading at the Vashon dock and chose Ted Olson, captain of the Ferryboat *Quinault*, as his best prospect. George kept one eye on the wheelhouse. When he saw the captain step outside and heard, "Here, George," the gull stopped casing the cars for handouts and flew to the boat. He landed on the stateroom directly behind the wheelhouse where Captain Ted held out chunks of bread for him.

The bird ate from the man's fngers. Sometimes Captain Ted called down to children on the deck to watch. They stared open-mouthed or said, "Ooah" or "Won't he bite you?" George wasn't put off by their noise. He was there for the business of eating.

The gull paid for his bread. He kept the other gulls away from the wheelhouse and upper deck. That is, until a senior gull came around reasserting his territorial rights, which didn't happen often.

The captain told George about the gull on the Tahlequah run who grew fond of peanut butter and jam, how the gull eventually turned up his nose at plain bread. George wasn't that fussy.

The gull had a good thing going. He cadged from Captain Ted for three years until the captain was transferred to the *Tillikum*.

The *Tillikum* and the *Quinault* worked the same run and sat side by side at the dock. On the morning of the transfer George flew to the *Quinault* to get his daily handout. He found someone new in the wheelhouse. Over on the *Tillikum*, Captain Ted called, "Here, George."

The gull flew to his friend. But, he didn't land. He circled the boat and eyed the captain. Still he didn't land. He circled the boat again, then returned to sit on the *Quinault*, looking sadly over at the new boat. No matter how many times Captain Ted called, he couldn't coax the seagull to land. The bird bobbed his white head this way and that way as if explaining what was wrong. The only thing the man could think of was the metal deck of the *Tillikum*—maybe the gull disliked it, or couldn't walk on it.

It broke up the friendship. Although others fed the gull, in a short while George disappeared. He abandoned ferryboat life, handouts, and his benefactor. But he was not forgotten. Captain Ted hung a picture of him in his house as a constant reminder of his favorite freeloader, Quinault George.

Told to Editor by Captain Ted Olson, Vashon Island, WA

A Merry Ride to the Ferry

It's only a fifteen-minute bus ride from the downtown Seattle ferry terminal to lower Queen Anne Hill, where I do my daily eight as a working stiff. But coming back down the hill in the P.M. can be another story. Late afternoon traffic through Belltown and past the Pike Place Market tends to snarl, especially in bad weather, when First Avenue gets as swarmy as New York's Delancey Street during a bagel giveaway. With just twenty minutes or so to make my ferry this can sometimes cause heavy stress, and palpitations, even.

So, it's Christmas time and snowing and when I board good old No. 18 one twilit afternoon, laden down with an armload of parcels, I steal a seat from a fresh kid in a cowboy hat and snatch a gander at my watch. We're already running late.

But don't shoot the piano player, as they say, he's doing the best he can. In fact, he makes up a minute and a half right away by finessing a red light at First and Denny.

We're on a roll from there till we hit a stop in front of a tavern just below the Millionaire's Club. This is one of those watering holes with "For Sale" paintings all over the walls. I'm just sitting there thinking maybe I should drop in one of those places sometime and mix a little culture with a few cool ones, when the rear door of the bus flies open. A guy steps up, but not all the way in, then he just stands there undecided like.

A woman sitting behind me yells, "Well, make up your mind!"

But he doesn't pay her the time of day. He's wedged in the open doorway like a stalled Mack truck in a shower stall, and he's conversing leisurely with a buddy on the curb. The guy on the step looks like he was just thrown out of a Nome, Alaska saloon. The back of his mackinaw is plastered with sawdust and icicles. But, despite the fact he's wearing a New York Mets baseball cap (sideways), I can't work up any sympathy for him. His friend on the snowy sidewalk is dolled up in a Sherlock Holmes deerstalker cap, with one earflap missing, and a flowered canary and chartreuse short-sleeved Hawaiian shirt. His arms and face are a shade bluer than Sinatra's eyes. The two of them are debating whether or not they should return to the tavern and take in some more art work.

The woman behind me, whose acquaintance I don't want to make, but who does have my sympathy, suddenly lets out a scream, "You clown, you're gonna make me miss my ferry!"

The guy in the wood-chip mackinaw turns and fires right back. "Who called me a fairy?"

But this is a bad move on his part, because he loses his balance and does a sloppy half gainer into the arms of his conferee. The piano player, always on the alert for such opportunities, slams the door prestissimo, and we're off again.

A glance at my watch tells me the minute and a half we made up at Denny has melted away, and on top of that we've lost another 90 seconds. The woman behind me is mumbling words I haven't heard since a friend of mine hit himself in the crotch with a mallet.

When we reach Pike Street a mob empties out of the bus in slo-mo, and another mob is trying to climb aboard as I eye the racing hands of my timepiece. I say they're trying, because a skinny creep in a studded leather jacket is now lodged in the front door of the bus, woozily chewing the fat with the driver, to the vocal displeasure of the woman behind me and the throng waiting behind him in the snow.

The piano player now displays a little artistic temperament. "Step back in the bus, Meatball! You're blocking the bleeping door!"

The twerp holds his ground in the doorway. In fact, he does more than that. Before you can say Casey Stengel, he unzips his jacket and pulls out a big horse pistol which he promptly sticks in the driver's ear. That revolver looks as old as General Custer's toenails, but the barrel's as long as a smokestack, and nobody's laying any bets it doesn't work.

"Don't shoot the piano player," I hear myself saying.

The runt chooses to ignore me. He seems to think the guy can do better and he's willing to give him one more chance. "We're all goin' to Pioneer Square," he snaps. "We're goin' fast, like no stops!"

The piano player keeps his eyes straight ahead on the sheet music. "Yes, sirrr!" he sings out with renewed respect.

He bangs the door shut, and the bus heads down First Avenue. Forget the red lights, we're going super-express now, right down to the wrought iron pergola and the big totem pole.

The lady behind me is muttering something like, "I don't believe it, I don't believe it!"

But I do. This is the Wild West, ain't it? Where men are men! I take another fast look at my watch and do some speedy calculations. We've already whizzed past my stop at Marion, but if this half-pint bravo gets off at the pergola, I still have time to grab my ferry by scooting down Yesler. And that's exactly what he wants to do, he wants out at the pergola. The driver slams on the brakes, throws the door open and the punk sails out and up the street toward the J&M Cafe.

I already have a quarter in my mitt which I flip to the fresh kid on the hang rail.

"The desperado's headed for the J&M," I yell. "Call the sheriff, Buckaroo—and you're a hero! Me, I got a ferry to catch!"

I grab hold of my parcels and hit the street running.

Richard M. West, Bainbridge Island, WA

Commuting

Old men
these boats
striding
in search of
the chair and the cups of
faces
that have papered their lives
daily departing   daily arriving.

Old instruments
these boats
continue to repeat
their course
yellowing
like ivory on piano keys
that never absorb
the players' sweat.

C. Hunter Davis, Vashon Island, WA

Twenty Cars Too Late

A commuter roared onto the dock at Winslow, twenty cars too late for the ferry. The hefty young driver jammed his gearshift into park, bellowed curses at the smokestack of the departing ferry, and pounded on his steering wheel. He got out, slammed the door of his pickup, opened it again and slammed, opened, slammed, opened, slammed. Next he walked around the car kicking the tires. Moving to the hood in a final gesture, he banged it with both fists. The noise reverberated around the dock. Finally he stomped off in the direction of the tavern.

Richard Braden, Bainbridge Island, WA

High School Commuting on the *Crosline*

Some of my fondest memories are of commuting to high school by ferry. The years: 1932 to 1936. The route: Manchester to Alki Point.

Our ship was the ferry *Crosline* and the only crew members I recall were Captain George Clemments and Mate Bob Vetters. Other classmates were Nona Denniston, Howard Grant, Jack O'Neill, and Bob Whitner.

Captain George allowed us in the wheelhouse one at a time. Frequently he let me steer the boat during the forty-five minute crossing. He also accommodated our tardiness. When he saw someone running hard for the ferry, he would bring the boat back to the slip. Sometimes, however, I had to jump across open water as the boat pulled away. Bob Vetters let me leave my mud boots in the engine room during the rainy season.

Our bunch spent very little time studying. The main activity was card games in the lounge. Only one student consistently used the time for study. That was Jeff Heath who later became a prominent major league baseball player for the Cleveland Indians.

During stormy weather our wide boat pitched violently from side to side as it climbed over the waves and plunged into the troughs beyond. Once, in the main salon, Bob started across to the other side of the boat at a steep angle. When the craft changed pitch, he couldn't reverse his lean and started running—winding up head and shoulders through the window glass, with no injuries.

Another time it was calm but very foggy. Whistle signals told the captain a tug and barge were near. After trading whistles for several minutes, we saw the tug. The ferry was directly over the towline. However, the tug's line was deep enough so that the ferry could proceed safely.

One morning we were called to the rail to see a small deer swimming on a line from Blake Island to Bainbridge, roughly four miles.

Those years ended far too soon. The *Crosline* ranks high in my commuting memories.

Howard White, Bellevue, WA

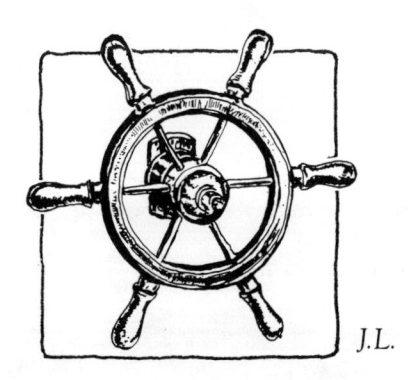

J.L.

Quiet! Please

The first run to Bremerton Monday morning is usually the quietest of the week. Commuters sleep or read newspapers; sailors returning from weekend parties catch some sleep.

One Monday morning a sailor was still partying, with his stereo blasting. A burly yardworker politely requested, "Turn it down." The sailor did, for a while.

The next time, the worker said, "Turn it down! I won't tell you again!" Quiet, for a while.

When the music reached blast proportions again, the yardworker grabbed the radio and heaved it overboard.

"Hey! That was my radio!" the sailor exclaimed.

"Turn it down," said the yardworker.

"You threw away my radio!"

The worker tapped the sailor's nose: "Turn if off!"

The rest of the trip was the usual quiet.

Robert Mize, Bremerton, WA

Wanna Bet?

George Green was a creature of habit. Every morning at 6:30 he parked his Datsun in the parking lot and boarded the ferry, drank coffee with Monk and the early-to-work crowd in the coffee shop. When the ferry docked, he raced with the gang for seats on the Metro bus parked by the ticket booth.

One morning Myrtle convinced him to take the car in order to meet her for a night on the town. He chortled when the deckhand waved his car into the best spot on the ferry—the middle lane.

In the coffee shop Monk pounced, "How much you bet on the Husky game tomorrow? I'll take Oregon. Come on, just five bucks." George mentally fingered the money in his wallet. Not again. Monk wasn't going to suck him in this time. He kept his hands around his coffee cup while bets were made.

At the sound of the landing whistle, George bolted from his chair, raced down the stairs and hurried up the ramp to the bus well ahead of the others. He rushed to the back seats and slunk down low with his newspaper in front of him.

Out of the corner of his eye he saw Monk push his way toward him. He groaned in defeat.

"Say George, isn't that your Datsun I passed on the ferry? All the cars are having to detour around it."

Told to the Editor by Jack Pennington, Vashon Island, WA

"*Now listen up, commuters— this is your skipper speaking. I want all of you to realize your potential today, stay away from sweets, don't forget your raincoats, and no dawdling on the way to the boat tonight. Over and out.*"

Susan Wallace, Bainbridge Island, WA

Quarters

Before putting Sally, her ten-year-old granddaughter, on the ferry, Dorothy Jones slipped a quarter into her hand. It seemed a nice way to say good-bye after the girl's week-long visit on the Island. When Dorothy's husband saw this, he slipped a quarter into Sally's other hand.

"Dorothy," he said, "there's nothing on the ferry for a quarter any more."

Told to the Editor by Dorothy Jones, Vashon Island, WA

Never Underestimate the Ladies' Room

I stepped into the Ladies' Room on the ferry. The long shelf under the wide mirror was covered with enough cosmetics to impress an Avon Lady.

The owner of these items gazed intently at her reflection, nose three inches from the mirror, while her deft fingers massaged cream into her face and neck. She picked up a soft flannel cloth and carefully wiped off the cream. She had barely started. Yet to go was astringent with its own little cotton balls for dabbing. Then there was moisture cream, peach blush, with appropriate applicator. Next was a box of powder with a puff; a little crock of rouge with puff; lipstick, eye shadow, and eye liner.

I stood behind her, attempting to find the part in my hair that had disappeared in the wind on the car deck. After a futile struggle, I left and found a seat near the rest room door.

Seconds before the ferry landed, she emerged. She looked like a star, her hair carefully frazzled all over her head, her skin luminous, her blue eyes staring through frames of black liner and false lashes.

Nine out of ten women rush out of the house every weekday morning leaving part of their grooming to finish on the ferry. On the boat, they dash to the Ladies' Room before anyone sees them in curlers and without make-up. Inside, they brush on nail polish and paint on lipstick—especially lipstick if they've drunk coffee on the way and left part of it on the rim of the mug. One or two crouch over the wash basins to floss and brush their teeth.

One day I found two teen-age girls chattering like birds as one wound permanent wave rollers on her friend's dark hair.

"How come? I asked. "Can you finish before the ferry gets to Fauntleroy?"

"Don't expect to," answered one. "We started this job in our beach cabin and all at once the water wouldn't run. So we picked up our stuff and we're going to her house in West Seattle. The timing's just right."

I heard a child cry once when I was sitting outside near this multi-purpose room. I jumped up and ran inside. There on the far side of the room a mother and auntie briskly rubbed down three little half-naked boys. A pile of soaking wet clothes made rivulets on the floor. Nearby an open suitcase held piles of dry clothes.

The mother explained, above the cries of the youngsters, that someone had recommended they take the boys for a ferry ride on this vacation from Kansas. On the Vashon side, the boys had waded along the shore to see what saltwater felt like. All at once big waves came. The first wave drenched the children. Before they got out, two more came, as big as the first one. Just then the ferry tooted for its return trip to the mainland. The women grabbed the kids and their things and tore down the dock, barely making the boat.

"Fortunately," said the mother, "we had these dry clothes." The middle boy cried and talked at the same time. He didn't want to be dressed in the Ladies' Room.

A week later I learned that little boys were not the only ones who changed from the skin out in the Ladies' Room. There stood a beautiful young woman without a stitch on, attempting to slide into panty hose while standing up. Worn jeans, a soiled T-shirt and frayed tennis shoes lay on the floor. She was well put together. Playboy centerfold would have snatched her up had they been fortunate enough to be there.

In a twinkling she dressed, looking preppy in her high heels, pleated skirt and soft green Italian knit sweater. She ran long fingers through auburn hair and asked the young woman next to her if she looked all right for a job interview.

"I overslept," she explained.

A teen-ager, with curling iron plugged into the wall, turned to the girl behind her, "Maybe I could get a job if I looked like that."

A young blonde came rushing in the door, saw her friend and blurted, "Oh Deb, am I ever glad to see you! I told Butch I couldn't go to Seattle today because we were having company. He's on this ferry. He's right out there. Would you go out and watch to see which stairs he takes? I'm breaking up with him. I won't move till you come back."

One day I was in the Ladies' Room to patch up my nail polish when a tall woman wearing a beige raincoat came in and asked in a low voice, "Anyone seen a woman with a red coat in here?"

At that moment a red-coated woman carrying a basket stepped through the door. "You Sadie Swanson? The lady who wanted the puppy?"

"Yes, I am. Is he in the basket?"

Just then a fluffy white puppy, with beady eyes and triangular ears sticking straight up, poked his head over the edge of the basket.

Sadie lifted the puppy carefully and nuzzled it against her chin and neck. "I love it," she said. "I'll take it. I've got the money right here." She counted out $250.

"I want one, too," I said longingly.

"This is the last one of the litter," Sadie said. "I saw her ad for West Highland terriers. I phoned and she said she'd be going into Seattle and if I'd take the boat to Southworth, we'd make a deal on the way back to Vashon."

Now the ladies' room is a pet shop. What next?

Blanche Caffiere, Vashon Island, WA

Sharon Munger, Vashon Island, WA

A Dollar a Hog, 50 Cents More for a Man

We naturally gripe about the cost of riding the ferry to Whidbey Island. Yet it's cheaper now than when fares were first collected—the same year the Civil War began.

In July, 1860, Thomas Coupe contracted with Mr. Thomas Smallfield of Port Townsend to build a 27-foot sloop to be used as a ferry between there and Whidbey Island. Mr. Smallfield agreed to have the sloop finished by October, but production delays, like ferry boats, have been around quite a while. By February of 1861, however, Whidbey was being serviced daily by this ferry, the *Maria*.

The boat, built at Smallfield's yard, had a centerboard that lowered to act as a deep keel for sailing close to the wind and raised to let Captain Coupe sail in close to shore. The passengers traveled in convertible luxury—the removable coach roof stayed behind on sunny-day crossings. But lean and yachty *Maria*, named after Coupe's wife, traded cargo space for speed. Described in an 1860 newspaper while being built, as "something undefinably grand and symmetrical," she ran the choppy seas off Whidbey under almost 150 yards of cloth. With a 36-foot mast, 30-foot boom, 13-foot gaff, and a 16 by 28-foot jib, this first ferry was very fast indeed.

Bureaucratic baggage found its way aboard and, at a May meeting of Island County Commissioners, rates of ferriage and freight were established on the run between Port Townsend and Ebey's Landing. A hog could ride for one dollar and a man for 50 cents more.

At Ebey's Landing on Whidbey Island The Ferry House was built for travelers. Offering spirits and a supper as well as bed and breakfast, this was an enterprise sure to succeed—a place to wait for the ferry. Not only was it more expensive to ride, but back then when you missed the boat you missed it by at least a day.

R. Wayne Strack, Whidbey Island, WA

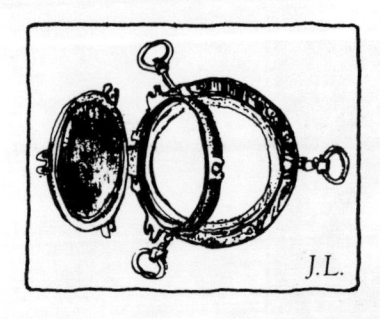

Greg Onewein, Bainbridge Island, WA

A Good Boat

I was working the extra boat, the *Vashon*, only survivor of the old wooden ferries, one Sunday in Summer after a four-day weekend. We came into Orcas to pick up a load of cars. The driver of one car declined to load, saying he'd rather wait for a "good boat."

Eight hours later, when we docked at Orcas again, this same man was happy to ride the *Vashon*. Every other boat that went by was full and had not stopped to pick up any cars at Orcas.

Robert D. Johnson, Clallam Bay, WA

Dismissal on the Seattle to Winslow Ferry Run

You dive. Back to the skyline,
you surface smooth. This distance
it is the shirt I know—color of bachelor
buttons and the pool where I never swim.

    It is only a trick of the wide ferry
    windows at midnight, the turning
    hour, but the thrum of the engines steady
    to the Peninsula, apart as an island.

You take the ocean as it comes, dark but never
still. Between cafes and lonely nights, high waves snag
the moon. I am close to losing decision,
your shirt rising and falling
like a voice, luring me to belief.

    My face reflected in the window
    rippling against the steeled
    and very-numbered city I'm leaving behind,
    this is the world between, the time
    for doubts. But like Morgaine hoping
    for the love of Lancelot, staying away
    from Avalon too long, I dare
    reflection: your shirt floating,
    buttons sinking past my hand,
    you folding me away, used, under
    your second rib.

Man of the sea, you keep no cupboards,
no mirrors, no magic. This ferry's throb,
deep in her bowels, has a life of its own.
I listen for the other side

    and wave, the ancient sign of goodbye.

Susan Landgraf, Renton, WA

Plans

Aboard the ferry,
the noise of killing time
surrounds us like exhaust.
In a video toy box,
missiles bombard cities
with electronic fallout;
a ten-year-old champions
the world for a quarter.
Cupid shoots his warhead
across matching T-shirts.
A commuter wears detente
headlines across his
three-piece suit; a comrade
tells him Seattle
is a prime target area.
Retired couples argue
vacation plans for returning
to the Nevada desert
in the Fall.

Where would you go,
my friend asks,
given a thirty-minute fuse?
Sirens in my ears,
I try to remember
when we left the dock
as sun stares
down mountains
through trees
across water
burns
into a million faces.

Linda A. Vandlac, Sedro Woolley, WA

Last Ferry

When Chet Hunter woke up he wondered where in the hell he was. Night pressed wetly against the windshield of his Vega, where he sat hunched over the steering wheel like a man hugging a life raft. As he slowly unbent and stretched his taut muscles he wondered how long he'd spent in that cramped position. The stiffness in his neck suggested an eternity. His head thudded dully. At twenty-two he was old enough to recognize a hangover when he had one, but this sense of dislocation was something new.

"Boy, did you tie one on tonight," he muttered out loud, hoping to dispel his confusion by naming its source.

With the cuff of his sportcoat, which he noticed was hopelessly wrinkled, he wiped away a patch of fog from the glass. As first all he could make out was a blurred mosaic of trees and the white blankness of mist. Faint moonglow animated the clouds. Ahead of the car and some distance downward Chet could make out light: a single bulb ringed with a spectral halo. He leaned forward. The light illuminated a sign, difficult to read against the glare, black letters on a white board that merged with the background of night and mist. It took a few moments of concentration for them to come into focus, to link together into words: Washington State Ferry.

"So that's where this is, the ferry landing." He heaved a deep sigh of relief. The evening was beginning to fall back into place.

He'd been out at the Sounder Tavern with his friends, Mark and Eddie, celebrating his imminent departure from "this loathesome speck of rock" on which he'd grudgingly resided for the last year and a half. His plan had been to catch the midnight ferry to the mainland, headed off-island for the last time.

A quick glance into the back seat of the car confirmed that everything was in order; it was filled to overflowing with all his worldly possessions. The luminous dial of his watch showed a few minutes before twelve. Just in time to catch the last boat.

Maybe my luck's changing, he thought hazily as he fumbled for the key in the ignition, and then turned it over. The Vega rattled into life with a cough. Somehow (he refused to let the "how" bother him) he'd gotten himself where he wanted to be just when he wanted to be there. He grinned in self-congratulation.

"About time I got some breaks in this crummy life. Once I get off this lousy rock I'm never looking back. I'm gonna make it big on the mainland: new job, new surroundings, get me a fine lookin' lady. The sky's gonna be the limit for me. Now if only the damn ferry'd be on time for once."

He settled back in the seat to wait. The purr of the engine was the only sound in the stillness. He played with the heater, getting it cranking. He switched on the radio, but after wandering awhile up and down its empty field of static, he shut it off.

He sat back up, wiped distractedly with his sleeve on the glass again. He tried snapping the headlights on and off a couple of times, watched the flare light up the fog bank, watched it fade back into blankness. Behind the pool of light at the end of the dock the wall of fog was dark as a cave mouth.

Chet leaned forward. There the ferry floated, waiting. When had it arrived? Why hadn't he heard it?

Yet there it was, undeniably, waiting at the end of the pier. Light splashed against its dark, glistening deck, the pilot-house stared blankly at him out of the mist. For a moment he hesitated, watching it, his hand on the parking brake. He had to squint to see against the bulb's glare.

A man stood in the puddle of light at dock's end, a thin man in a black skipper's uniform, his face shadowed under the hat's sharp bill. Chet put the car in gear; released the hand brake; let it roll down the short decline onto the dock. He came to a sharp stop beside the ferryman.

"One way, and glad of it," he crowed as he tossed his coins into the thin and bony hand, staring derisively into the deep shadows under the hat's brim. "Not much business tonight, huh? Hardly pay you to run it."

"You always take this one alone," the old man replied as he stood back to let the car pass.

Chet chuckled as he slid down the lip of the dock onto the car deck of the ferry. Funny old guy, he thought. He pulled the car up aways and parked it. Wonder what that remark was supposed to mean?

The clank of chains echoed hollowly in the empty car deck as the gate was drawn shut behind him. He was surprised to find that his was the only car in sight. He opened the car door and began to clamber out, his heart strangely pounding. Then he noticed something that made him stop halfway out of the door. No wonder the ferry had looked dark and forbidding—it was painted the wrong color. Other ferries of the fleet were a uniform white with bright green striping. Every part of *this* ferry—walls, railing, deck—was a dull and lifeless black. What kind of ferry was this?

He stood up quickly and spun around, stumbling as he turned. The ferry had already begun to move. The island disappeared, lost in the mist and darkness, the dock light vanished as though it had been turned off. And then there was only the black water rushing by underneath him.

John Damon, Port Townsend, WA

Greg Onewein, Bainbridge Island, WA

Departure

Somewhere across the water lies
an island that comes and goes
at the whim of the unsettling mist.
I wait here for the ebbing beat
against my skin to rise into a gentle
humming. Instead my heart pulses
salt water, its leaky valve jerking
irregularly through the cycle.
It shakes this house of seas.
Rain slashes where ripples dissolve.
Foam roils like froth along bared fangs.
Confusion squeezes me tight.
The stars are lost behind my eyes.
The starboard leans to port.
The windbreak windows rattle
like words incessantly matching act
to schedule, coin to deed.
My mind rattles like a snare. Where flows East?
Where West? The huge barge roars
under its breath then treads water
while behind us the black city rises
like a dying dragon. I've been waiting
for days, watching the weather change.
As diesel under pressure builds
and explodes, I struggle from
the wooden piling where water breaks
beneath the prow—or is it stern?
and wade head-high into the darkness
that hides the moated castle asleep
under restless, slumbering waves.

Lonny Kaneko, Vashon Island, WA

The Host

Clad in khaki, formal white
and boardroom gray,
the many-eyed soldiers march
hurling fiery shafts
captured from the sun.

The moat of rippling blue water
keeps them at bay
until silent army meets trembling craft,
satisfying, for a time,
the appetite of City.

Len Elliott, Auburn, WA

Vashon Hot Heads

    It was the Vashon "hot heads" who launched the State of Washington into the ferry business. Following World War II, the Puget Sound Navigation Company was caught between rising operating costs on one hand, and public resistance to higher fares on the other. The situation kept the company in continual contention with unions, and with the State Legislature, which sought to hold fares down. Each time there was a strike, islanders were isolated, and with each strike they became increasingly aggravated. Finally, they organized a ferry district and obtained an exhausted ferryboat. When the Puget Sound Navigation Company lost an appeal in the courts, and was ordered to lower rates, the company tied up its sixteen boats. Captain Alexander M. Peabody, president of the company, stated that even the Supreme Court couldn't force him to run a money-losing operation. The act stranded an estimated 1,000,000 ferry users all over Puget Sound, but not on Vashon-Maury.

    If Captain Peabody had expected Vashon-Maury Islanders to plead for service at any cost, he was disappointed. The Vashon Ferry District put its little old ferry into operation, and when Puget Sound Navigation sought to return to the island, vigilantes wouldn't let the vessels land. The Vashon Ferry District, thereafter, operated a commendable service with a couple of small, worn-out ferries that barely survived frequent Coast Guard inspections. The District Commissioners continued the service until the state took over the ferries in June, 1951, a total of three years. No one was happier than the Commissioners, however, when they finally got out of the ferry business.

Excerpt from Isle of the Sea Breezes *by Roland Carey, Seattle, WA*

The Popcorn Caper

One morning a friend and I boarded the *San Mateo* at Vashon on our way to a Seattle TV station for an interview about our Community Players' upcoming production. We went into the galley for a snack. As we stood by the popcorn machine I rummaged through my purse for a coin.

Oops! My eyebrow pencil flipped into the overflow funnel. I could see it down among the kernels. Without hesitation I reached in, grabbed it, and then—uh,oh!—couldn't pull my arm back out. My friend pulled, a passer-by pulled, the girl behind the counter pulled. Then she greased my arm with butter and we all pulled again. No luck.

By now a crowd had gathered to point and giggle and offer suggestions, none of which worked. Finally a woman said, "I'll get the captain."

That did it. In short order the captain released the door, the funnel, and me. My entrapment over, the crowd dispersed.

At the studio before the interview I explained the grease and the Band Aid. Once on the air, to my embarrassment the emcee suggested I describe my recent misadventure to the viewers. Those viewers included my neighbors, my sons, and my camera-ready husband, who captured the moment with a snapshot.

Returning home that afternoon, I found a giant bag of popcorn on top of my mailbox. The attached note from a neighbor said, "Well, if you're that desperate for popcorn, this should do it."

Garland Baker Norin, Vashon Island, WA

Whistles

Landing and departure whistles are different:
   Landing: one long and two short blasts.
   Departure: one long blast.
When vessels are passing the following signals are used:
   One short blast: "I am altering my course to starboard."
   Two short blasts: "I am altering my course to port."
   Three short blasts: "I am operating astern propulsion."
Other signals:
   Five short, rapid blasts (at least): danger.
   Many toots that do not make sense to the layman: probably a boat drill.

Captain Glen Willers, Maury Island, WA

Tolkien Rides the Ferry

My level of distress is rising. Right there in the Vashon Island ferry parking lot where my truck always is, it isn't. Let's see now, upper row right, there on the flat by all the other vehicles with faulty parking brakes—no, it's definitely gone!

"Ssss, sss, gollum. Nassty, creepsy thieveses. They doesn't like us preciouss, they steals our lovely, rusty, mossy, preciousss truck. Sss. We'll sneaks up from behind and squeezes 'em, we will!"

This week my mind is being held hostage in J.R.R. Tolkien's world of hobbits, orcs and wizards. Maybe now the fantasy is spilling over.

Why would anyone steal a '59 Dorf panel? Exhaust pipes trailing on the ground, big rip in the hood where the dismembered fan blade came flying through, doors that crang like thunder—who'd want it? I must have parked in the upper lot this morning.

Huff, puff, ssss, puff. Nope, not here either. Strange. Wandering back to the lower lot, I watch how the ferry cuts a white swath in a field of blue. Beautiful. Beautiful, but strange. Strange but . . .

"Curse us and crush us! My truck is on that boat!"

Arrggh. Blast you, Tolkien, you sweet-writing devil, you! Now I recall. Thirty minutes ago I drove onto the ferry, then climbed upstairs with *The Hobbit* to escape off into the Misty Mountains with Bilbo, Gandalf and Gollum. Twenty minutes later, as I had for a thousand days of commuting on foot, I walked off the boat, visions of wizards dancing in my head.

A red flush sweeps into my cheeks and ears as I retrace my steps back down the dock. Gad, how do I handle this one? Sss, sss, gollum, gulp.

"Uh, excuse me, er, how does one retrieve a panel truck when it is, uh, inadvertently left on a ferry that is headed back to Seattle?"

The usually pleasant ferry person has no smiles this time. She makes a call, then lets me sweat it out. The mighty, mossy Dorf will either be pushed off at Fauntleroy or halfway between here and there.

"It's the smelter fallout," I venture, "Decays Islanders' memory cells like maggots in cabbage."

In my case she'll believe that.

Finally the ferry is back and there she is, grand and glorious in her moss coat, locked up tight and impassively dominating the center aisle where the other cars have been painstakingly navigated around her. I try a lame smile at the two deckhands, but there is no mirth in Middle Earth.

As I open the door the "craangg" echoes down the center steel cavern. The starter whirrs a few times, then growls, catches, and she coughs to life.

Ah, yes. Just another day of Island commuting.

Frank Jackson, Vashon Island, WA

Landings

The currents at Tahlequah Landing can be bad when the tide is going out on a big ebb. While a ferry waits in dock for ten or fifteen minutes, the current may change directions two or three times and run with terrific velocity in the opposite direction each time it changes.

Coming into the dock at Tahlequah is difficult to plan. It's possible to miss a landing even after you've done everything right. People ask, "Who's the dumb skipper? Where'd he get his license?"

The ferry is the only ship that comes into dock bow first, which makes it more difficult. All others come in alongside the dock.

Many ferry runs may have as few as eight landings during a watch. The Point Defiance-Tahlequah run has about eighteen landings. The Fauntleroy-Vashon-Southworth Run has twenty-eight.

Captain Glen E. Willers, Vashon Island, WA

Shaw Island Landing

On the way to Orcas one dismal, wet March morning, our ferry pulled into Shaw Island. Until that morning, we hadn't heard of this island.

As the ferry approached the dock, we saw a tiny figure in long brown skirt and shirt jacket lowering the ramp, struggling against the full force of the wind. When she finished the job, she wiped her brow. By then we were close enough to see that the ramp attendant was a nun.

We made inquiries and learned that on Shaw Island the Franciscan Sisters of the Eucharist run the dock agency, the nearby gas station and the general store. They shun publicity, are self-supporting, and do their good works privately.

The last person we saw that morning, as our vessel pulled away from Shaw Island, was the little nun, cranking the winch that raised the ramp.

Joan Bellinger, Burnaby, B.C.

Judith Lawrence, Vashon Island, WA

The Honeymoon

We were the first to board the ferry. Twisting the gold band on my left hand I walked ahead of Charlie toward the front deck.

"We'll have to get that sized, Jess, before you lose it."

I nodded.

Settling into a deck chair, I watched the first rush of water as the ferry plowed a course toward the San Juan Islands. The hot summer sun soaked into my skin.

I felt the steady rhythm of the engines below me. A bird, silhouetted against the noonday sun, swooped through the sky. A gust of wind lifted the hair from my neck.

With a start I turned. Charlie was standing above me, a curious light in his eyes. His large hands rested on the back of my chair.

"What's the matter, Jess? It's only me."

I squinted up at him. My husband. This was the man I had promised to share my life with. For the past few days I had seen something new in him each time we talked—or touched. Something hard and cold, almost calculating.

He sat down next to me on a deck chair. His long fingers played with my hair. I felt his breath, warm on my cheek, as he leaned near me.

I stared out over the water. The shimmering waves undulated.

Charlie shifted in his chair.

"I think I'll walk a bit." His eyes, blending with the blue of the sky, made me dizzy with their intensity. With an effort I turned away. Had I changed or had he?

We had traveled for days, along the jagged bluffs of California, along the foggy Oregon coastline, and finally into the brilliant Washington summer. Our honeymoon.

Closing my eyes, I drifted with the rolling waves. Unconsciously, I twisted my ring until it slipped off my finger and fell to the deck with a soft ping. My eyes flew open and I watched in fascination as it rolled to a stop at the feet of a tall Indian woman.

Her gaze was piercing as she held the ring out to me. I stood slowly, moving toward her. Our hands touched lightly.

She was as dark as I was fair. A thick braid with a single silver streak hung down her back. Her flat nose contrasted sharply with high cheekbones, the dark skin marked with a fine network of lines. She wore a long skirt the color of moss and a black jacket embroidered with a red eagle's head. What was she doing on this ferry I wondered, among the tourists in shorts and sundresses.

"I live at Friday Harbor," she said.

Her voice was low and husky. I guessed her to be around sixty.

"Sixty-seven, to be exact." Her dark eyes twinkled.

Startled, I placed the ring back on my finger.

"You don't have to leave, my dear." She gestured slightly. "Pull your chair near me. We must talk."

Wordlessly I did as she suggested.

"I've been watching you. You're troubled."

I looked around for Charlie. Where was he?

"He's at the other end of the boat," she said in her low voice. "We have plenty of time."

Before my lips could form the questions, she answered.

"I do healing and psychic readings. I seldom intervene in someone's life but I sensed such a strong rush of anguish from you that I had to speak."

While I digested this piece of information the woman sat serenely, her wrinkled hands folded loosely in her lap.

"I'm here to help you."

I stood clumsily, knocking the metal chair to one side. My legs felt heavy. I wanted to move away, but couldn't.

The woman smiled up at me.

"You can go any time you want to."

I sat with a thud. A light sweat broke out on my forehead.

"Why me?" I asked weakly.

At that moment a cloud blocked the sun, shrouding us in gray.

She shrugged. "We were brought together."

I took a deep breath. "I was just married. This is my honeymoon."

Glancing at my ring, the woman frowned. "I know."

"Do you know Charlie?" I asked.

She studied my face solemnly. "I know only you. Search for your true feelings and follow them. Your dismay is well founded. Trust yourself."

I stared at her in disbelief, then stood, dazed.

"You can't know."

The woman looked at me steadily, her eyes like round chestnuts.

"You are wrong," I said lamely, walking away.

It was hot and stuffy inside the cabin and I choked back tears. Tears of what? Rage? Hurt? Fear? Where was Charlie when I needed him? He was always there when I didn't need him, hovering over me, suffocating me with his presence.

I went into the restroom, and stared at my reflection in the mirror. Some honeymoon. I exhaled, splashing cold water on my face. Bending over the sink, I watched drops of water roll off my chin.

I don't love him. My heart thudded in my chest.

It's all a mistake.

I looked bleakly at my water-stained face, patting it dry with the coarse paper towel.

Out on the front deck the woman was gone. In her place was Charlie, his long legs crossed at the ankles, his sun-faded shirt hugging his shoulders. "Hey, Jess, come on. We're about to dock." As he stood, his eyes stared straight through me.

I swallowed hard. Goosebumps covered my arms and I twisted the ring, first one way then the other.

How will I tell him, I wondered.

The boat bumped the side of the pilings and shuddered to a stop.

Kathryn Park Brown, Santa Barbara, CA

The Blink of an Eye

We were parked on a side lane four car lengths from the front of the ferry. A decrepit truck was stationed in the center aisle at the head of the line. I had stayed in our car instead of going to the upper deck as my Dad and the rest had done.

When the ferry slowed to dock at Fauntleroy, most of the travelers came downstairs and entered their cars—all except the driver of the truck. A deckhand removed the wooden blocks wedged against the wheels of the first vehicles. Then he stood up front, his back to the truck, waiting for the ferry to dock.

At the moment my Dad reached our car, I noticed a slow forward movement of the truck, still without its driver. It was rolling straight at the deckhand, gathering momentum.

I tried to yell but panic made me speechless.

Dad saw me pointing. He whirled around and shouted. The man turned just in time to see the truck heading toward him. He ran back to the truck, wrenched open the door, and pulled on the emergency brake.

This drama took place in the blink of an eye. When the truck driver appeared, whistling gaily, no one said a word to him. I doubt if he ever knew how close to disaster he had come.

Marybelle Craig, Seattle, WA

Clyde

Clyde was one of those dogs almost everyone liked immediately. He was not too big and not too small, with a coat of black, brown, gray, and white short hair. Tail wagging, smiling, ready to be petted, he approached total strangers as if they were long lost friends. His eyes were amazing. One iris was bright blue. The other was half blue and half brown.

Clyde lived on Lopez Island with Barnes. Barnes rode his bicycle more than he drove his car, and Clyde would run along after him for miles. Often Clyde would join a group of off-island cyclists and run with them for part of a day. Sometimes he'd go off visiting other dogs and people while Barnes was washing dishes at the Islander.

One summer Barnes went to Alaska with several other friends from the island to kill fish on a purse seiner. Clyde stayed with John and Donna until he wore out his welcome by fighting all the time with their golden retriever. Then Dan, the bicycle man, kept him at his house. Because Clyde was such a roamer, he was kept on a long leash. Sometimes Dan would unhook him so he could go visit his friends. This leniency led to a great adventure for Clyde and trouble for Dan.

One day, gregarious dog that he was, Clyde joined a group of cyclists and followed them to the ferry landing. When the ferry came, Clyde got on board too. When the boat reached Anacortes, the cyclists rode off, leaving Clyde behind.

"Whose dog is this?" the purser and deckhands asked when everyone had left.

"He got on at Lopez," someone remembered.

"We'd better send him back!"

Clyde did not get off at Lopez. He stayed on the ferry until it got to Friday Harbor. There he wandered around town, meeting people, until he was arrested by the sheriff for being "At Large."

He was taken to the dog pound. People looked at his tags and made several phone calls to Lopez until they finally got in touch with Dan.

"Clyde is in the Pound," they said. "You have three days to come and get him or he will be destroyed. And you have to pay a $50 fine."

Dan went to Friday Harbor and arranged to go to Court. Then they rode the ferry back to Lopez, and Dan kept Clyde on his leash until Barnes came back from Alaska. In Court, the fine was finally lowered to fifteen dollars.

Next summer Barnes went to Alaska again and Clyde disappeared without a trace. A lot of people missed him. Barnes said he wouldn't be surprised to see Clyde on the cover of *People* magazine someday.

Peter Fromm, Lopez Island, WA

Night Ferry
a group poem by 5th graders, Wilkes School, Bainbridge Island, WA 1981

When you ride on the ferry at night you can see the stars and moon.
The ferry is going over the shiny blue waves,
the ivory boat and silver engine sliding over the waves.
I feel cool and relaxed when the ferry is going at top speed.
On the ferry at night you look out the window and see the buildings light up.
Sometimes all you see when you look out the window is pitch black water.
When you go out on the deck and smell the fresh sea air
you can hear the waves crashing against the ferry.
I see the seagulls flying low by the splashing waves.
At night the ferry looks like it floats in space.
At night you see other ferries passing and giving you waves so you fly.
At night the moon is like a yellow night light glowing in the sky.
I see dark blue wavy water going by.
The moon is a cue ball glowing on a black pool table.
When I look at the moon on the ferry I wish I could sleep on the moon
and make it my home. The moon is a golf ball
over the blue ice cold water and the big waves.
The moon is a green apple on a black piece of construction paper.
The moon seems to just about fall on the boat.
One night I saw the ferry rise up and fly past the moon yelling ha ha ha ha.
On the ferry you can smell the salty air and the smell of food in the cafeteria.
After about halfway I wish I could be at the other side or I could have 25¢.
On the ferry I see, hear, smell, and taste the food.
On ferries you can see and hear video games.
I see the people closing up the cafeteria as the kids play video games
and the dads read the newspapers.
On the ferry I smell the steamy aroma of crisp french fries.
I like to hear the buzzing and blipping of the video games.
You can see the lights in Seattle, and you can eat in the boat too.
You can hear the motor go faster and faster.
Their cookies are as big as flying saucers
and the average time for a video game is 3 hours!
The video game kills us off when we go on the ferry.
Never ever eat their clam chowder because it tastes bad.
On the ferry the clam chowder is made with cyanide.
I see colored lights from shore.
The ferry is like a boat on blue air.
It's dim and very exciting as you're bumping along.
The ferry begins to jump on rocks.
The waves look like monsters trying to swallow the ferry.

The ferry is a bucking bronco that can't be tamed.
The ferryboat is a trackless cable car.
I can see the ferryboat go down in the middle of the trip.
The boat is sinking, everyone is running. Under the seats people reach for life jackets.
The ferry takes off from Seattle and halfway through it dives like a petrel and dies.
On the ferry it's noisy and windy and people are being blown off.
The ferry is flying upside down like an earthworm being thrown out of a bird's mouth.

Hita von Mende, Vashon Island, WA

Jasmine

With fast-moving parents like Tressa and David AspiriHakala, Jasmine decided on the day she was born to land on her feet and establish her own way of doing things.

Her parents had planned to leave Vashon July 1st for a camping trip to Blake Island, but Jasmine put a stop to that. On June 30th at 8:15 she announced her imminent arrival by sending vigorous labor signals. Tressa called a midwife, Margaret Smith, and a photographer, Shirley Ferris, for the planned home delivery.

Margaret paled when she examined Tressa. Jasmine had done a complete reversal since the last exam and was now coming down the birth canal feet first. Time to call in help: Stan Horan, Paramedic; Dr. Jim Lenhart, M.D.; the Aide Car; and an alert to the ferry that an emergency trip to Swedish Hospital on the mainland was underway.

Jasmine had other plans. She was coming and nothing slowed her—not the bouncing of the Aide Car as it rushed along the highway; not the bumping as it shot down the ramp onto the *Klahowya* at 12:10. With Daddy David and Mama Tressa working together through each contraction, the baby was born, feet first. This little "footling breach," as her Mom called her, drew her first breath on a Washington State Ferry twenty-three minutes after boarding.

Ordeal over and baby safe, the parents insisted they wanted to go home. When the ferry landed at Fauntleroy, the Aide Car swung around on the deck and got in line for the return trip to Vashon.

Jasmine Charlotte's birth certificate reads, "City of birth: *Puget Sound*; hospital or birthplace: Ferry *Klahowya*." This name is the Indian word for "Welcome."

Tressa AspiriHakala, Vashon Island, WA

Ferry Unlikely

Like caterpillars
ferries move,
munching water
into foam.
Do they ever
metamorphose
into seaplanes
and fly home?

      Mary M. Webber, Seattle, WA

      Ann Alexander, Sedro Woolley, WA

On a Slow Ferry to Victoria

The words tasted cold that day as the wind
blew them back to us, tugged at our hair,
pushing until it seemed we stood
in one position while the shores
of Bainbridge and Whidbey Island pulled slowly
away. It could have been another
time with the lighthouse on the promontory,
standing tall and smooth like a pillar
of salt; the dolphins arching their backs,
looping the sky and water. Still, I could see
the skyline of the city, the buildings blurred
with the distance we had travelled.
Above us, a seagull folded wide wings,
beginning the long dive under. I think
I said, *Remember* but it could have been
Don't look back. You shook your head
instead of speaking, watching white beads
of our breath mingle with the bow's spray.

      Sharon Hashimoto, Seattle, WA

Who Needs the Ferries

About once every ten years, after the summer days have drifted away and fall leaves become mash on the sidewalks of Puget Sound cities, someone will propose that bridges, hovercraft, or hydrofoils replace the picturesque green and white ferries of Washington State.

These suggestions spread across Seattle and Tacoma newspapers when fog and rain tend to obliterate the vistas from the deck of a ferry. If time-saving ways to cross Puget Sound were publicized in bright Summer or Fall, passengers aboard the ferries would perceive such suggestions as practical jokes.

The Washington State Ferry System operates twenty-two vessels of nine classes serving eight Puget Sound routes. These boats carry over eighteen million passengers a year: daily commuters, merchants hauling supplies, and tourists.

Thousands of campers, hikers and foldboaters choose the Summer and early Fall to explore natural wonders in Western Washington. One of the heavily used ingresses to these wonders is via the Washington State Ferries.

Olympic National Park consists of two large hunks—first, the rugged interior mountains, and then, to the west, the long ocean beach shaped like a salamander. Both include thousands of acres of untouched natural beauty. Yet this great park and hundreds of other smaller state, county, and municipal parks are easily reached by riding a ferry across Puget Sound.

Once on board, cyclists, backpackers, and RV families may witness various sideshows to further enrich their journey. Whales, seals, and sea otter offer exciting deckside entertainment. Overturned sailboats are rescued by ferries. Occasionally a passenger will change his mind, leap from the car deck, and swim back to the dock. Suddenly-awakened drivers have been known to roar over the side for a dunking or into off-ramp walls and abutments. In July, 1975, a brave athlete water-skied for two miles on a towline leading from the *Hyak* on the Seattle-Bremerton run.

Failed equipment and bad weather have led to crushed ferry docks and boats run aground. These highlights, however, are the exceptions. In 1985, the Washington State Ferry System accurately boasted of "a 34-year record of safe transportation service."

Less dramatic inboard adventures have also marked the recent history of Puget Sound ferries. Business law courses were taught aboard the Bremerton-Seattle run. Groups have rented the vessels between service runs for marriage ceremonies, dances, art shows, and music recitals. It is not uncommon to enjoy folk or chamber music while on a cross-Sound trip.

The upper decks, most with contour benches or chairs, offer mid-Sound playpens for reading, sun-bathing, inhaling clean breezes or nuzzling. From July through September, backpacks and sleeping bags are piled against topside bulkheads.

It has been about ten years since the last serious push was made to scrap the ferries. With Winter upon Puget Sound, soon someone may rise like a phoenix and declare that the glories of modern technology demand more modern, speedier modes of transportation.

A counter view will then surface and the familiar strange bedfellows will gird for battle: commuters, environmentalists, history buffs, old-timers, and backpackers.

One must experience personally this fleet of clean, green and white vessels that silently, almost insolently, cruise back and forth across one of the few natural inland seas of America. Then it is easier to understand why whizzing hovercraft or the arched girders of a bridge can never replace the natural, measured rhythm of a cross-Sound ferry.

Junius Rochester, Seattle, WA

What the Captain Does

When the departure-time arrives, but before a Washington State Ferry pulls out, certain checks are made in the interest of safety. The *Evergreen's* captain, identified by four gold bands on the sleeves of his navy blue uniform, stands by in the in-shore pilothouse waiting for a signal from the vehicle deck that loading is complete, the safety chains spanning the ferry's outer ends are in place, and the tie-up lines taken in. He also makes sure the first officer is in the off-shore pilothouse. With a pilothouse on each end, the officers have better vision in docking, undocking, piloting and ship-handling—also having a propeller on each end simplifies maneuvering. The ferry doesn't turn around, she is always going ahead.

To get the ferry underway, the captain signals starting orders to the engineer standing by at the engine room motor controls. Two diesel engines, of 1,250 horsepower each, drive generators supplying electricity to the two propeller-driving motors, and the engineer and the oiler keep continuous watch on all the machinery to make sure no failures occur.

After the routine checks, the captain enters the departure-time in the logbook, and slowly starts the ferry away from the slip, sounds a warning blast on the horn, and gives the first officer in the outer pilothouse complete control. When clear of the land, the officer increases the speed to thirteen knots and the slight increase in vibration tells the passengers they are fully underway. (Captains tell us that the procedure is similar in the super-class ferries.)

Excerpt from Ferry Story *by Mike Skalley, Seattle, WA*

Hita von Mende, Vashon Island, WA

The Last Crossing

The *Klahowya* made its umpteen-thousandth uneventful landing on the Seattle side and disgorged its cargo of autos and trucks which departed with a clonkety-clonk of tires over the gangplank.

As the *Klahowya* lay cradled by the pilings, Henderson pondered his years of service. He had devoted most of his life to the Washington State Ferry System, to the green and white slugs that trudged and slithered up and down Puget Sound.

He'd always told his wife he hated the job, was just putting in time until retirement. Now, as the deferred pleasures beckoned—Hawaii for two months, then some honest-to-goodness furniture making—Henderson looked around with a tinge of sorrow. Tomorrow this wheelhouse, grafted on his soul like a barnacle, would be a dimming memory. To make things worse (God, they always did this) they had scheduled the usual: cake, coffee, with "a little something extra" added between conspiratorial winks, and the present everybody pitched in a buck for. Contrived hoopla at the last bell. He had almost called in sick.

A deckhand below gave him the high sign and, after Henderson pulled away from Fauntleroy, the first mate took control of the ferry at the opposite end of the boat.

"The way they build these slugs, you can't call either end a fore or an aft," Henderson said to the empty room.

Pretty soon it's Miller Time, he thought. Then he remembered the scarcely concealed preparations of the crew for his "65 and out" party.

He locked the door, opened a paper bag and pulled out a fifth of Ancient Age. He never drank on the job, but what the hell, all he had left to do was skipper another run from Southworth to Vashon, then Vashon to Fauntleroy.

In one hour Captain Henderson would have his farewell present, his cake, his trip to Hawaii, his rendezvous with homecrafted furniture—and oblivion. Sitting on the floor, head propped against the door, he took hefty gulps from the bourbon. As the ferry left Vashon, he sang snatches from Wagner's *Gotterdammerung* in a lusty tenor.

At Southworth, he took the wheel once again for what was to be his last pendulum swing to Vashon and back to West Seattle's Fauntleroy dock. Now his Wagnerian arias were punctuated with bellows of self congratulation—"Brilliant! Grace under pressure! Bold One!"—clearly audible to the crew, who had gathered for his party.

Cries of "Hey, open up, Hal!" and "What the hell are you doing?" mingled with the joyous strains of "For He's a Jolly Good Fellow" and shouts of "Surprise, surprise!"

What happened after that was hard to explain. Henderson swung the boat north, while the crew banged on the windows, some in delight, others afraid of losing their jobs, others in fear of a disaster at sea. The few passengers who had boarded the *Klahowya* seemed unconcerned about when or if the ferry was going to land.

The crew caucused and decided not to break the door or a window to gain access to Henderson. It would be easier to blame the off-course meanderings of the ferry on malfunctioning machinery than it would be to fill out forms explaining intentional damage to State of Washington property. Above all, nobody was sure if going berserk during the last hour on duty deprived one of a lifetime of accumulated benefits. There were those present who were of a mind that it did. The vote was close, but all democratically abided with the majority's decision: let Henderson run amok until the shift was officially over.

The *Klahowya* steered a steady course up the Sound, past Magnolia and on to Edmonds. The 9-to-5's waiting for the *Klahowya* on the Seattle side made nasty phone calls to People in Power, mumbled about moving permanently to the mainland, or drove off for hamburgers at McDonald's and a sixpack at the 7-11.

The passengers on the *Klahowya* assumed a disaster had struck the Fauntleroy dock, forcing them on to downtown Seattle, then to Edmonds, for a safe harbor.

As Henderson, sweat and glee painting his face, roared at the top of his lungs his favorite arias from *The Flying Dutchman*, the crew was called away from their vigil over Henderson at the wheelhouse door to put out a bonfire set off in a passenger's pickup truck. After the blaze was finally extinguished, a magical sense of community spread to all on board. Life had been suspended.

Henderson steered the ferry past Whidbey Island, past Port Townsend, on a course for the Pacific.

The crew signalled "no danger" to a hastily summoned Coast Guard cutter. With no sign of distress or mutiny, and no Higher Authority demanding the vessel's seizure, the Coast Guard sailed off in huffy dignity.

On her way the vessel went, her captain transported in a crazed Germanic frenzy of song and laughter.

Tales of spotting the *Klahowya* mark her at times as sailing near the Bahamas, or off the Siberian coast, or anchored in Tahiti, where you can charter her for a day's run at sailfish. Others say she went aground near La Push where she was quickly cut and salvaged by an embarrassed Washington State Ferry System.

The last anyone heard, they were offering no rewards for her recapture.

Larry Johnson, Vashon Island, WA

Keys!

Patty rummaged through her bag. "My keys! I've locked them in the car!" She gave me an "Oh-God-what-do-I-do-now?" look, and dashed for the stairs. We were on the *Walla Walla*, Winslow to Seattle. I sat remembering the last time she'd locked her keys in the car. It took two men and a policeman to get a window open. Would we ride round trips for the next two hours?

But Patty was back, smiling. "I found a deckhand and told him what I'd done. 'No sweat,' he said. 'Happens all the time.' I showed him my car and he said he'd bring me the keys."

And he did, ten minutes later, keys jingling in his hand, a grin from ear to ear. We thanked him profusely.

"Never miss," he bragged.

Martha M. Richards, Port Townsend, WA

A Cluster of Grapes

Joan Wickham from Vashon, a gourmet cook and professional food stylist, prepares display food for shows, TV programs, and advertisements.

Regular Vashon commuters know Joan's Trans-Am and recognize when she is carrying food to her shows by the delightful aromas that escape from her car.

One day Joan prepared for a TV show featuring ways to create fancy breads. In her trunk sat a display of miniature rolls designed to look like a cluster of grapes. Joan had brushed a golden glaze over each "grape" and had tinged with green the stem and leaves that encircled the cluster. The display was attractive and the smell of the baked bread tantalizing.

As usual Joan went up to the passenger deck for a cup of coffee. Returning at departure time, she noticed the trunk of her car was not well closed so she slammed it shut. She seldom locked her car on the ferry.

Half an hour later she realized why the trunk had been unfastened.

When she slid the tray of rolls under the lights of the TV camera and removed the wax paper from her creation, she found that the stem was in place, the leaves were there, the bottom crust was intact, but every "grape" had been plucked from the cluster.

Told to the Editor by Joan Wickham, Vashon Island, WA

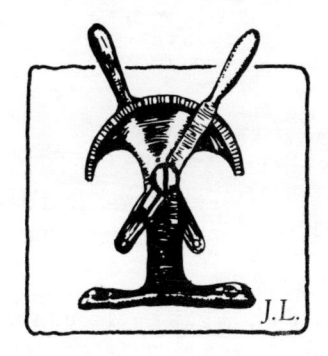

San Juan Tail

We sailed west from Anacortes, nearing Lopez Island. Before we pulled into port, the ferry started turning. The ferry continued to turn and we found ourselves headed back the way we had come.

Suddenly the loudspeaker came on. "Passengers, please check your dog if you brought one on the ferry. There is a dog overboard." Everyone rushed to the railings and watched as the ferry chugged in the direction of a black head, barely visible in the distance. The dog was swimming toward shore.

As we approached, the ferry slowed and the owner of the dog whistled. The big labrador reversed his direction and swam toward the ferry. A gallant deckhand with a pike pole hooked onto the dog's collar and hoisted him aboard amid great hurrahs from the passengers crowded around.

Jessie Winn, Shaw Island, WA

Babysitting on Puget Sound

One rainy Sunday in Seattle I was blessed with four lively grandchildren for the day. Suddenly a bright idea dawned. We would take a "mystery trip." Chattering excitedly I hurried them down to the waterfront where the big ferryboat *Walla Walla* was docking. As we boarded I warned them not to climb the railing.

Finding a mid-way point on the passenger deck where I could count bobbing heads, I spent a pleasant afternoon enjoying the scenery, the waters of the Sound and the mountains beyond.

Three crossings later, four exhausted children and one well-rested grandmother watched a rainbow curve over the Smith Tower while bidding a happy good-bye to the world's largest floating playpen.

Mae Swofford, Seattle, WA

Letting Go

We stayed in the car that night, neither of us wanting to go up on deck as we normally would. This was not a festive occasion. We were parked in the middle of the ferry—no view, nothing of interest to look at, just one another.

Perhaps this would be good. We would talk. My son and I had not talked in some time. We'd done a lot of yelling, but not much talking.

He'd been in trouble at school. When he turned sixteen we finally gave up and allowed him to quit. He said he would get a job. He hadn't. He spent the days lying around the house, the nights hanging out with friends, smoking pot.

So we threw him out, our first born, his father's pride and joy, the apple of my eye. I'd spoiled him, even more than his sisters, allowing him, practically from infancy, every possible opportunity to "express his individuality," as I was fond of putting it. He would grow up self-assured, an original thinker, successful. My plan appeared to have backfired. Maybe on his own he'd get himself together.

He'd lived with friends for about a month when he called to say he had a job on the peninsula near Port Townsend. He'd be living there. The Hood Canal Bridge was still out. Would we take him to Kingston on the ferry and drive him to Lofall where he would take a ferry to the other side? He'd hitch a ride to Port Townsend from there.

I volunteered to go. My husband was too angry. I imagined them "having it out" on the ferry, then careening wildly along the rain-slicked highway to the Canal. I could handle it more calmly.

I glanced at him as he sat beside me. He'd insisted on finishing his cigarette in plain view of the "No Smoking" sign. He could be so maddening. If there was a rule to break, he would do it every time. He finally put it out with an annoyed smirk in my direction.

"Thank you," I said.

"Whatever," he mumbled. I watched as he adjusted the rubber band that held his long, braided hair in check. He took such pains not to identify with his father, the doctor, whom he referred to, not altogether lovingly, as "Mr. Straight." No chance of mix-up here.

He wore a favorite outfit, faded yellow T-shirt with a hole in the middle, plaid flannel shirt with a torn pocket, ill-fitting, stained bomber jacket and frayed jeans. "I just want to look like an ordinary guy, not some rich kid." Bingo.

"You hungry?"

"No, Mom, I *told* you. I *ate*."

"You've got everything you need?"

"Yeah."

"Money?"

"No problem." He stared off into space.

So much for our talk. I leaned my head back and closed my eyes. If only he'd *say* something, I thought—express regrets or even allude to some plans, no matter how vague.

He said nothing.

I listened to the sound of the engines and the rush of moving water. I found myself remembering all the times we'd taken this ferry since he was a baby. All the vacations, the day trips. I pictured him at the age of three bounding from the car up the stairs to the main deck. He'd stop at the candy machine, then race out toward the bow, his father in tow. I saw them standing at the railing, my son a round-faced, feisty kid in a hooded sweatshirt. I heard his loud, high-pitched voice over everything.

"What kind of duck is that, Dad?"

"What kind of boat is that, Dad?"

"How many fishes are there in this ocean, Dad?"

Passers-by looked at him, then at me, and smiled.

His father answered each question with such patience, pointing out from time to time the approach of a distant freighter or a deadhead rolling on a nearby wave. Any father would have done as much for a future Summa at Harvard.

And now, this.

I looked at him again and caught him staring at me.

"What are you thinking, Mom?"

"I was thinking of all the times we've ridden this ferry."

"Right on, me too," he grinned. "We had some far-out times."

After landing at Kingston, we drove to the Canal in silence. The ferry had just pulled in as we arrived at the loading area. He removed all his gear from the car, muttered something about keeping in touch and headed toward the dock. Cars started to stream off. He stood waiting for the last one to pass.

I watched him with a lump in my throat. He hadn't looked at me. We hadn't hugged one another. He seemed so young as he stood there in the rain with the wind blowing the brim of his old red hunting hat.

I wanted to call to him, to tell him to come back, that we'd go home and somehow sort things out. But I knew I had to let him go.

Then, as he was about to disappear into a crowd of foot passengers, he turned and waved. I rolled down the window and waved back.

"Hey, Mom," he bellowed, his voice carrying above every other sound, "I love you."

"I love *you*," I screamed back.

Passers-by looked at him, then at me, and smiled.

Janet Appleton, Alderwood Manor, WA

Elegy Without Grief
assignment for Marvin Bell's poetry workshop, Port Townsend, 1983

1. The ferry I would have, boat of the lazy
   irrepressible mind, carries
   the red shoulder or blue heel
   of some constellation.
   If she has gender, or moves too slowly,
   it is because of the forces against her.

2. No one said it would be easy.
   The ferry left and returned,
   it took centuries.
   I thought I was awake.
   If the ferry returns
   while I am sleeping I don't want to know.
   There are people
   I can't have, pasts that travel
   without knowledge of the present.
   If you were here, I'd show you
   how to go slow, how to be
   the only moving object in a scene.

3. This is the last thing I will say
   about the ferry. When she is gone
   the whole arc of the journey
   denies itself. While I stand and watch,
   and do not stop her,
   or know why I want to.

4. Once I lived on the ferry,
   ate ferry food and drank expensive
   ferry drinks. The sea was mine
   and the world was small
   because I moved across it. I could see
   land, and the girl who stood
   with my name in her white nightgown,
   in her uncurtained window.

Judith Skillman, Bellevue, WA

George Wright, Vashon Island, WA

Missing the Ferry

That morning on Vashon
I ran for the ferry too late.
Out of breath on the dock,
I watched that white boat
floating out to Seattle in silence,
turned back to your beach,
to your vine-covered deck,
fresh brewed coffee
you served in a blue and white cup:
was it Japanese, Chinese?
You showed me photographs, drawings,
a rug with two dragons.
In the window
the 10:30 ferry appeared.
On the path, wild red berries to taste:
name forgotten, not ripe.
Then the foghorn,
the clang of three flights to the rail:
you were already fading away on the beach
like a driftwood, a seaweed,
like sand in the wind.

Lee Dhyan Owens, Seattle, WA

Jon Rader Jarvis, Vashon Island, WA

Journeys

If there is spring rain on the wide panes of the ferry windows, and if I can hear the clinking of coins in the vending machines, then the ferryboat once again becomes magical.

Every May, my family left the wintry city and rode the ferry that led us into the wonderful world of Summer at our beachplace. We locked up a house full of bus tickets, rain boots and oil furnaces, and piled bicycles, swimming suits and cameras into a rented red truck.

On the ride across I studied the information on lifesaving vests and bought Lifesavers with hoarded nickels that clattered as they rolled down the metal candy machines. As I pressed my nose against the window, stained with winter rain, Summer grew closer and closer. Then, just as we reached the dock, it appeared as if a rainbow.

Nothing could go wrong on this island of wild blackberries and hummingbirds. I spent most days following families of crabs along the sand or building cone huts underneath the cool Douglas firs.

Five times a day, an old steel hulled ferry, the *Kalakala*, passed our house. It had been dubbed "The Silver Slug" because of its snub-nosed bow and its achingly slow bulk. It was not at all well liked among commuters, but I loved it.

As it passed by our beach, books and figurines would fall out of shelves and some adults would lose their teeth. It left enormous waves that my sister and I believed were the twenty-foot surfing waves of California. Shivering in Puget Sound, we paddled out on air mattresses and waited as the waves gathered force. Just as they approached we would kick and go furiously for a free, somewhat unsteady ride to shore. In the evening the *Kalakala* lit up the water like a floating birthday cake. I could feel its pound in my chest as I went to sleep.

"The Silver Slug" retired and my sister and I grew up, not, I am sorry to say, to become surfers. Instead I went away to college and spent Summers working in the city. The dreaminess of childhood evaporated as I awoke to alarms instead of sunshine on leaves, and as I concentrated on my major and career in lieu of barn swallows and wild sweet pea.

Then late one Fourth of July, I arrived at the dock to find it bulging with holidayers. Irritated that I would miss a traditional picnic, I was only slightly aware that the relief boat was an old steam powered boat. I was anxious for some fresh air when I finally boarded and made my way to the deck.

The night was warm and very clear. All around, fireworks from boats and land exploded in patterns. And from above, the smokestack let off wafts of metallic steam that landed on my shoulders. The odor stayed for a long time, and I began to relax. As I stood there with the salty air getting cooler and the sky flashing, I realized how important the magic of childhood was as I entered the serious business of becoming an adult.

C. Hunter Davis, Vashon Island, WA

Judith Lawrence, Vashon Island, WA

Fitting
for my teachers and coaches at Marshfield High School

The *Hyak* rips a crooked seam
across Elliott Bay,
tears its facing apart
and slaps tangled foam
into November wind.
Marking the pleats of wave
between this boat and shore
gulls tack
above the ravelling gray crests.
They dart low over
the flapping eyes of water.
Their savage weaving
shapes a pattern.
Tailors
who cannot judge proportion
would say, "Too much gray."
But men only drop
their stitches into time.
It is the flight of gulls
which pulls our cloth
into perspective, from dawn
to the final fitting.

Tom Erdmann, Jr., Seattle WA
Previously published by Folly Press, Tacoma

Susan Wallace, Bainbridge Island, WA

Contributors' Notes

ANN ALEXANDER lives a fairly simple life with her cat, downwind of a dairy in Sedro Woolley, pacing the floor, waiting for fan mail and orders for postcards.

LINDA ANDREWS lives in Kirkland, Washington with her two children. She is a member of Northwest Renaissance, a non-profit coalition of poets, publishers, and performers. Her poems have appeared in various publications, and she was a featured reader at the 1985 Pacific Northwest Arts and Crafts Fair.

JANET APPLETON is a published writer of poetry, fiction, and articles. Wife of a Seattle physician and mother of four grown children, she is now putting the finishing touches on her first novel. First Place, Stories: Nightwriter Contest.

TRESSA ASPIRIHAKALA and her husband, David, are Vashon Island residents. Both attended Evergreen University. Tressa runs Puddle Stompers, a Day Care Center. David was Joyce Delbridge's student in sixth grade.

DARSIE BECK, Northwest marine artist, is a Vashon Island native who attended San Francisco School of Art and is best known for marine illustrations and sculpture. He lives with his wife, artist Christine Beck, and their four children on Maury Island.

JOAN BELLINGER is a freelance writer specializing in local travel, history, and poetry. She has been published in England, Canada, and the U.S.

MARGI BERGER is a Wisconsin transplant to the Northwest, happily watered and rooted. A registered nurse from Yale, her career has included medical writing, editing, and literature search. Her poems have appeared in numerous publications.

CATHARINE HOFFMAN BEYER teaches in the University of Washington Interdisciplinary Writing Program and takes Nelson Bentley's poetry workshop. She has published poems in *The Oregonian* and has won poetry awards in Oregon and Washington.

RICHARD B. BRADEN and his family live on Bainbridge Island near historic Port Madison. An aircraft and missile design engineer by trade, his avocation is building and repairing wooden boats.

KATHRYN PARK BROWN successfully ran a bed and breakfast business for five years and is now living in Santa Barbara, California. She recently completed a romance and is now working on a full length novel. She is a founding member of Vashon Island Nightwriters.

BLANCHE CAFFIERE is a little, young-in-spirit lady living with husband, Cy, at Burton on Vashon. After teaching forty years in Africa, England, Oregon, and Washington, she is now writing a book with Garland Norin on early families on Vashon.

ROLAND CAREY lives in West Seattle and is a maritime historian. His books are *Isle of the Sea Breezes*, *The Sound of Steamers*, *The Steamboat Landing on Elliott Bay*, and *The Sound and the Mountain*.

STEELE CODDINGTON of Bainbridge Island is a Vice President of Merrill Lynch subsidiary Family Life Insurance Company in Seattle. Writer, poet, mountain climber, and horseman, he wrote a column for the now defunct *Enetai*, was a Winslow City councilman, and now enjoys life as a wine connoisseur.

LAURAN COLE recently spent two years living and working in Japan. She is an honors graduate of the University of Washington Creative Writing Program. Her nephew Marshall, now three and an experienced ferry rider, greets even the tourists and charms even the nappers.

MARYBELLE CRAIG spent her teenage years on Vashon, then moved to Bremerton, married, and had a daughter eight days after she contracted polio. In 1979 she retired after thirty-three years of government service. Her hobbies are writing limericks, traveling, and contacting her classmates for reunions.

JOHN EDWARD DAMON has published over seventy poems but this is his first short story. He teaches Spanish and English at Chimacum High on the Olympic Peninsula. He and his wife are expecting their first child.

C. HUNTER DAVIS wrote her first poem on her sneakers during a tennis lecture in gym class. The shoes were damp from walking the tidelands of Puget Sound. Not much has changed: her shoes are still full of seawater, her tennis is non-existent, and she is still writing. Nightwriter member.

HARRIET ORR DAVIS, native of Nashville and graduate of Vanderbilt University, lives on Bainbridge Island half the year. Her poems have appeared in one anthology and in local publications including *Island of Geese and Stars*. She has studied with Nelson Bentley and with Beth Bentley at the University of Washington. First Place, Poetry: Nightwriter Contest.

JOYCE DELBRIDGE and her husband, Bill, moved from Burien to Vashon's waterfront sixteen years ago. Since retiring from teaching in 1979, she has been engrossed in a professional writing career with three juvenile novels in the works, as well as newspaper articles, and publicity for theatrical productions. She also teaches a writing workshop and is a Nightwriter member.

MICHAEL DEVOE, a painter and sculptor specializing in marine life, has lived on Vashon Island for fifteen years, painting, making furniture, and doing wood sculptures. He is now working on a series of "tidal chairs" using marine subjects.

LEN ELLIOTT, a freelance technical writer from Auburn, Washington, has published poetry in *The Disciple* and *Triangle Review* and short humor in *The Wall Street Journal*, *Reader's Digest*, *Tacoma News Tribune*, and elsewhere. His puzzles and word games have appeared in *Games* magazine and Dell Champion publications.

TOM ERDMANN, JR., ever since he was just a little zipper, has kept everyone in stitches. His fondest ambition is to publish a book of poems done entirely in needlepoint on fine linen. His other fondest ambition is to get his faithful wife of sixteen years back to work, to supplement his miserable income as a Seattle high school teacher, so they can afford to send their three sons to advanced weaving classes.

HAL B. FERNANDEZ has kept a journal of poems since 1967, writing "hundreds of pages on the ferries." He attended seventeen schools before graduating from West Bremerton. His poems have appeared in various publications, including *MS Emissary*, the Puget Sound newsletter of the MS Society. He has worked for thirteen years as a flight attendant with United Airlines.

PETER FROMM is a freelance photo-journalist living on a 30-foot wooden sailboat based on Lopez Island. A graduate of the University of Oregon and Ohio University, his favorite pastime is beachcombing.

PAUL HALVORSON, a Northwest native, claims he has spent thirty-eight tumultuous years getting "here." He has no plans of turning back now.

SHARON HASHIMOTO lives with Emmett, her chocolate Labrador Retriever, in south Seattle. Her work has appeared in *Amazella*, *The Arts*, *The Seattle Review*, *Gathering Ground*, and elsewhere.

JACQUELINE FLOTHE HILLSTROM remembers the old quote, "None but a mule can deny a family," but with much laughter and apologies she keeps trying. She was born in Tacoma, but like a gaggle of Canadian honkers her family moved to and from Alaska the better part of her life. She now paints her memories of Alaska at her home in Sequim.

KRIS HUTCHISON is a sophomore at Bainbridge High School. Besides writing, she is in the Debate Team, the Math Club, and the Spanish Club. But most of all she enjoys just being hyper with her friends.

JEAN ISABELLE IVERSON, when not "globe tottering," lives in her Burien studio house among paint daubs and dribbles, glass shards, stray grace notes, and bottles of correction fluid. She has published children's stories and in *Resources Magazine* and has illustrated coded booklets of nursery rhymes.

FRANK JACKSON is a Vashon Islander who is sporadically overcome by an uncontrollable urge to write. Earlier seizures resulted in *Practical Housebuilding for Practically Everyone* (McGraw Hill, 1985).

WINIFRED JAEGER spent her early years in Brooklyn, grew up in Berlin, studied piano in New York City, and after twenty rich years in Santa Barbara, settled in Kirkland, Washington. She works as a legal assistant to a maritime attorney and also teaches and plays piano, recorder, and viola da gamba.

JON RADER JARVIS, Vashon Island artist, is a graduate of the University of Washington with degrees in printmaking, painting, and engineering. He works with watercolor and acrylic. Vice President of Vashon Allied Arts, he was in charge of the 1984 Strawberry Arts & Crafts Fair on Vashon Island.

LARRY JOHNSON, a lawyer, lives on Vashon Island with his wife, three children, a pony, a goldfish, and assorted dogs and cats. Working in Seattle, he is grateful for the Puget Sound moat that surrounds Vashon, and for a ferry system sufficiently inconvenient to keep newcomers away. He writes "The Computer Corner," a monthly column for the *ABA Journal*.

ROBERT D. JOHNSON grew up in Anacortes. He worked for Washington State Ferries through high school and college and for three years prior to entering Seminary. He has been a Presbyterian pastor for the past six years and is now serving a congregation in Clallam Bay.

JERRY-MAC JOHNSTON is an actor, poet, playwright, and children's book author. In addition to his creative efforts Jerry-Mac is one of Seattle's most eligible unlisted bachelors.

HANNAH JONES studied art at the University of Oregon. She has illustrated for magazine articles and for *Wild Harvest*, a book of edible plants. She is currently working on folk paintings of Eagledale, Bainbridge Island.

PEGGY JULIAN lives on Bainbridge Island, has a partial view of Puget Sound, and rides the ferries to most of the places where she wants to go.

LONNY KANEKO, Vashon Island resident and widely published poet, has received a grant from the National Endowment for the Arts. Brooding Heron Press will soon publish a chapbook of his poems. Also a playwright, he co-authored *Benny Hana*, a play produced in San Francisco and Seattle. He teaches at Highline College.

SUSAN LANDGRAF is a poet (published); freelance writer and photographer (formerly a reporter); grandmother (twice); graduate student (University of Washington Creative Writing Program); and collector (of almost anything).

JUDITH LAWRENCE, owner of the late author Betty McDonald's home on Vashon Island, recently illustrated Marjorie Stanley's book *Historical . . . Sometimes Hysterical . . . Rhymes of Vashon-Maury Island*.

JANET LONERGAN is a native Northwesterner (moss behind her ears! webbed feet!) who lives in Bellevue with her husband, three children, and two cats. She writes juvenile novels.

MARY MACAPIA, an artist currently working in watercolor, usually paints flowers. However, she felt a killer whale was as worthy a subject as a blue delphinium. She has ridden Puget Sound ferries all her life, and also ferried to the islands of Mull and Iona in Scotland, and to Inishmore in Ireland.

DAVID B. MCCREARY came to Seattle via South Dakota, upstate New York, North Carolina, Minnesota, and the Marine Corps. He is a direct marketing consultant.

MARGARET D. MCGEE lives in Seattle with her husband, David, and David's hamster, Snookums. Employed as a technical writer, Margaret writes articles, fiction, poetry, and song lyrics as well as technical documentation. Third Place, Poetry: Nightwriter Contest.

ASHLEY MCNOOT, whose other name is Knute Berger, M.D., is an artist and research pathologist who lives on Bainbridge Island and had a cabin on Shaw Island in the San Juans for many years. A native Northwesterner, he tends to see this part of his world, its activities and people (including himself), in cartoons.

ROBERT MIZE (married, age forty-two, four sons) commutes by ferry to a nuclear engineering job at Puget Sound Naval Shipyard. He writes prose, poetry and "prosetry" for pleasure. Second Place, Anecdotes: Nightwriter Contest.

SHARON MUNGER, graduate of Miami University in Ohio in Art Education, lives on Vashon Island with her daughter, Rochelle, and son, Josh. She taught art in Vashon High School and elsewhere. She works for UP and squeezes in time for art when she can: metal work, batik, and watercolor.

GARLAND BAKER NORIN, a freelance writer, operates a collectibles shop, Spindrifters, in Pike Place Market, Seattle. She has a B.A. in speech and M.A. in Theater Arts from Washington State University. For forty-five years she has lived on Vashon Island, where she and her late husband, Sam, a KOMO-TV engineer, raised their sons, Robert and William.

GREG ONEWEIN, Northwest native, teaches art and American history at a Seattle alternative school and spends his spare time in and around the water. He lives aboard a houseboat in Eagle Harbor with his wife, Jill, and sons, Haven and Harte.

LEE DHYAN OWENS is a freelance writer and resume consultant. She has been a disciple of Bhagwan Shree Rajneesh for four years, and is now involved in bringing the Results Course to Seattle through her work with TNI (The Natale Institute).

ERIC PERRET is a student at the University of Washington who, as a small boy, would throw bottles with messages in them off the ferry.

MORRIS H. PIXLEY, a retired tugboat engineer and ferry worker, started at age fourteen and retired at sixty-two. For twenty-six years he worked for Foss Tug Company with fifteen years as chief engineer of the yacht *Thea Foss*.

HARRY PROCTOR was introduced to sailing by Henderson Camps on Lopez Island. Even at age eleven Harry knew there was no other life for him. After a drama degree and a stint as a navy fighter pilot he finally built his own 26-foot sloop, continuing the pursuit of his first love—sailing.

R.M. REDDING has lived most of his life in Alaska, with intermittent visits to Seattle. He is a writer by avocation, with several books in print, one a history of Boeing. He now lives in Sequim.

NANCY REKOW lives on a Bainbridge Island farm, has four children, publishes poems, teaches creative writing and poetry, has self-published several books (with Elizabeth Zwick); and works as a writing consultant/freelance editor.

SARA REKOW lives in a cabin on Bainbridge Island with her wolf-Malamute puppy, Hopi. She is a waitress at the Streamliner Diner in Winslow. Besides writing she likes to garden, bake, sew, run, and study anthropology and psychology.

MARTHA RICHARDS, University of Washington secretary and native Seattleite, retired to Port Townsend in 1972. Her interests are travel and painting, with freelance writing the latest. Third Place, Anecdotes: Nightwriter Contest.

JUNIUS ROCHESTER, freelance writer and regional historian, is a frequent state ferry passenger. A graduate of Whitman and of Harvard Business School, he is a member of the Pacific Northwest Historians' Guild and the Washington State Pioneer Association.

STEVE SAUL has lived most of his life on Vashon Island. In sixteen years with Washington State Ferries, he has worked on most of the runs. At present he is a Marine Technician in the engine room.

MIKE SKALLEY has worked for Foss Launch & Tug Company for the past fifteen years, and is currently manager of Seattle Customer Service. He has published three books: *Foss, Ninety Years of Tow Boating*; *A Medal for Marigold*; and *A Ferry Story*.

JUDITH SKILLMAN was born in Syracuse, New York, of a physicist father and mathematical mother. She has been writing since she was nine. Her work appears in *The Arts, Poetry Northwest*, and elsewhere. She teaches through the Continuing Education Program at Bellevue Community College.

PETER L. SMITH has lived all his life in the Northeast until July, 1985, when he moved to Redmond. He combines hiking and fishing with photography, creative writing, and his career in transportation and communications planning (now for Boeing Computer Services). He rode his first Puget Sound ferry (hence the poem title) in May, 1985. Second Place, Poetry: Nightwriter Contest.

TOM SNYDER lives in Indianola and works for the Washington State Ferries. He has studied poetry with Howard McCord, James Bertolino, and Madeline DeFrees. His poems have been published in *Dilligaf*, *Abraxus*, *Fragments*, and elsewhere.

REVA SPARKES, a Vashon Islander, teaches calligraphy, writes personalized poetry, paints, and is a charter member of Nightwriters of Vashon. Reva was a counselor for twenty-six years and now helps create living agreements for couples seeking clarity in their relationships.

BILL SPEIDEL lives on Vashon Island with his wife, Shirley. He operates Pioneer Square's Underground Tours in Seattle and is publisher of *Seattle Guide*. Among his published books are *The Wet Side of the Mountains*, *Sons of the Profits*, and *You Can't Eat Mt. Rainier*.

R. WAYNE STRACK is a writer of historical accounts and short fiction. A graduate of the University of Washington, he is a long-time resident of Whidbey Island and a member of the Puget Sound Maritime Historical Society.

MAE SWOFFORD worked for twenty-five years at the Olympic Hotel in Seattle. Now retired, she writes, travels, and extricates herself from things she signs up for. She says, "This is the first writing I ever signed, sealed and delivered on time and it won a prize. So there is hope for everyone." First Place, Anecdotes: Nightwriters Contest.

LINDA A. VANDLAC is a Bainbridge Island expatriate who now lives in the woods northwest of Sedro Woolley. She currently teaches writing and creative writing at a Job Corps Center.

HITA VON MENDE is an artist with home and studio perched on the north end of Vashon Island. Her oil portraits and landscapes have appeared in the galleries of Vashon and the homes of her friends. Her set designs have graced the stages of several Vashon community theater productions.

SUSAN WALLACE has commuted on the Winslow ferry since 1971, and has been a closet cartoonist for a lot longer than that.

MARY M. WEBBER, Seattle writer/consultant, is the original creator of "The Uncalendar" and a keen observer of the unscene. A literary butterfly, she alights at random on ad copy, TV commercials, arts promotion, and some serious stuff like editing and designing books.

RICHARD M. WEST, product of an unorthodox education, has been soldier, tinker, iconoclast, writer, beachcomber, and acolyte saint—not necessarily in that order. Banished from his native New York City, he is currently pursuing vice in the Puget Sound area.

HOWARD WHITE served as an Air Force transport pilot in World War II. Returning to the Northwest, he attended the University of Washington and spent thirty-five years as an engineer in the Manufacturing Department at Boeing. Now retired, he lives with his wife, Betty, and daughter in Bellevue.

KATHRYN E. WHITE of Seattle ended a thirty-year career as an educator to write for an audience she knows well. She usually writes make-believe, because children from two to ninety-two listen to her fantastic lies, then ask for more. She is working on *Trouble on Brady's Mountain*, a novel for young adults.

CAPTAIN GLEN WILLERS (Retired) lives at Dockton on Maury Island with his wife, Lorraine. Twenty-seven years in the ferry business, he worked first for the Black Ball Line, then the Vashon Ferry District, and finished with the Washington State Ferry System.

JESSIE WINN was born in Tacoma and raised in Western Washington. At age thirty she went to work overseas to support a son. She met her present husband while in Guam. They retired from Illinois to Shaw Island twelve years ago.

GEORGE WRIGHT, mother of two children, lives in Vashon overlooking the ferry dock. An assistant at City Arts Foundry, she experiments in slumping and fusing glass. In her studio she paints and does wax work.

ELIZABETH ZWICK lives on Bainbridge Island with husband, Peter; daughters, Kris, Katherine, and Hanya; and baby son, Michal. She is currently wrapped up in family, homemaking, and design projects.

FREDRICK ZYDEK, a widely published poet, has been running Matthews Bookstore in Omaha, Nebraska. He is a native son of Washington.